Kevin McAleer – **POSTDOC**

Kevin McAleer

POSTDOC

THE FOREIGN AND OTHER MISADVENTURES OF A NE'ER-DO-WELL SCHOLAR

Palm**Art**Press
Berlin

This is a novel, hence a work of fiction, and all its characters and institutions and other official entities are products of the imagination. Any resemblance to persons living or dead and institutions thriving or defunct is unwitting and purely coincidental.

Bibliografische Information der Deutschen Nationalbibliothek
Die Deutsche Nationalbibliothek verzeichnet diese Publikation in der
Deutschen Nationalbibliografie; detaillierte bibliografische Daten sind
im Internet über http://www.dnb.de abrufbar.

ISBN: 978-3-96258-088-9

Cover Design: Catharine J. Nicely
Layout: NicelyMedia
Druck: Schaltungsdienst Lange, Berlin

PalmArtPress
Pfalzburger Str. 69, 10719 Berlin
Publisher: Catharine J. Nicely
www.palmartpress.com

Printed in Germany

This book is dedicated to the memory of

ALLAN MITCHELL

1933-2016

I can't help wondering why I've lived,
for what purpose I was born.
There must have been some purpose,
I must have had some high object in life,
for I feel unbounded strength within me.
But I never discovered it.

Mikhail Lermontov, *A Hero of Our Time* (1840)

*

To be truly challenging, a voyage, like a life,
must rest on a firm foundation of financial unrest.

Sterling Hayden, *Wanderer* (1963)

1

When I returned to L.A. from Berlin that first day of December, I had half my dissertation finished. The Wall had fallen three weeks before, but I'd been so busy writing on nineteenth-century German dueling that I missed the event. The story behind that was I had gotten an extension on my research grant but couldn't extend my apartment lease so had to go through an agency which found me a short-term place in the Fasanenstrasse just off the Kurfürstendamm. The Fasanenstrasse was full of boutiques and jewelry stores like a mini-Rodeo Drive, the sixth-floor apartment cost me a fortune to rent, though it would have been lots more if the place weren't being renovated. That's why I had obtained the apartment at such short notice – it was barely habitable – the small bedroom equipped with just a table and chair, a cot-bed with a thin jailbird mattress, and some weird Bauhaus seat that was too ungainly to sit in and just took up precious space in the corner. I had been loaned a paint-spattered cassette recorder by an artist friend, but its radio reception was broken and the apartment itself had neither TV nor telephone, so I was isolated from the outside world and could now get my writing done with zero distractions. Also good was that the Fasanenstrasse had everything for the man who had everything but little for the likes of me, so the outside world didn't even tempt. If I was on a roll then for days on end I wouldn't leave the apartment, which had a bathtub that was long and deep, fit for a Roman emperor, a real luxury that turned into a necessity as reward for good work and a way to break up the day into halves or thirds or even quarters.

I had found the secret to unmatched productivity: get an upscale flat, preferably one you can't afford, then work your tail off day and night to justify the expense.

I'd been soaking and writing over the course of several days when I finally set foot on the street – my food supply had run out – and found they had opened the Wall.

72 hours prior.

All my history-writing had prevented me from experiencing history in the making, which seemed symptomatic, though I wasn't sure of what.

And because that writing had been done on a typewriter, now back in Los Angeles I had to transfer it to a word processor, so my sister loaned me hers. I'd never used a computer before, at least not for a sustained job of writing, and kicked things off by composing a 58-page chapter on the mechanics and protocol of the duel straight onto the computer, and neither saved the chapter properly nor made a hard copy, and one day tried calling it up and the chapter was gone.

Three weeks down the tubes.

That's when I reached for the bottle.

The alcohol tamped down my distress as I quickly rewrote with the material still fresh in mind. I worked morning, noon and night and powered through the holidays, ten days later I had 51 pages that were better and tighter than the lost 58, so I decided to do this for the whole dissertation.

Not lose the first draft – but drink.

Though I would have drunk anyhow. The academic game was getting to me. It was getting to me and I hadn't even finished the dissertation. Much of my weariness came down to the fact that I knew too many PhD students and too many post-PhD students called professors to be impressed by the degree. In my judgment the two smartest history grad-students at Zafiro Tech had meantime bailed on the program, which itself was proof of their smarts since they were too cerebral to be happy in the role of exalted drudge. They knew they were sharp cookies and didn't have to prove it through three post-nominal letters. You came across those who did. Like the housewives who wanted something to do after the kids had flown the nest and needed to feel they hadn't been dumbed down all those years with their brains on homemaker auto-pilot. The truth was you didn't have to be a so-called intellectual to get a PhD since it was just application, endurance and follow-through. Endurance was the main thing, like running a marathon, which for some perverse reason had become the gold standard of athletic achievement for would-be athletes. Any non-paraplegic could train for a period and reel off a marathon in four or five hours. I ran a marathon! I ran a marathon! What they called "ran." Race walkers covered the distance in just over three hours, so how about running one under three hours, not even good, just a fair amateur time, very few could swing that.

I got a PhD! I got a PhD!

Yeah but how quick.

Next day, after completing my mechanics-of-the-duel chapter, I cracked the screw top on a jug of red Gallo wine. This eased me into the task at hand – that task being to organize a coherent narrative on the duel's political dimension. I had spent so much time collecting my research material in Berlin's Geheimes Staatsarchiv that now I could barely bring myself to look at the stuff. But roused by the wine I overcame my aversion and my brain started humming at such a pitch that it drowned out the nagging analytic voice so assiduously cultivated in grad school and broke down all that fussbudget academic prose and within two weeks the BGS chapter was in the can.

My parents were at work all day, so I could indulge my bibulous routine, and afterward I would get cleaned up and gargle with Scope to make a reasonably sober impression when they returned home in the evening. Weekends were obviously trickier. And they weren't stupid. Suspicions can be excited after chugging half a gallon of burgundy, no matter how expertly concealed.

One morning I went to my computer and found a brochure from Alcoholics Anonymous laid across the keyboard. Inserted in the brochure was a questionnaire *Are You An Alcoholic?* I sat down with my glass of red and took the test, which I passed with flying colors, since just three yes-answers to the twenty questions meant "you are definitely an alcoholic" and I had NINE yes-answers. But the salient questions so far as I was concerned – "Do you lose time from work due to drinking?" and "Has your efficiency decreased since drinking?" – were answered with a resounding NO.

My work rate had never been so efficient, not even compared to the Fasanenstrasse stint, so I refilled my glass with the sense of a weight being lifted since I'd been having my own qualms about the boozing and was glad to put those fears to rest. But I braced myself for the discussion which was certain to ensue at dinner when all family issues were aired. After my nap I didn't drink for remainder of the afternoon, then in the evening I shaved and showered and got dressed in something other than a grungy sweatshirt and boardshorts.

"Steven, we think you're drinking too much," said my mother. "Did you see the brochure? Did you take the test?"

"It says I'm an alkie three times over."

"Oh Steven, we thought as much!"

"It also says the first stage of alcoholism is denial, so if I admit to being one then maybe I'm not."

"Or you're just in the advanced stages," growled my father who plunged a blob of mashed potatoes into his mouth then speared some string beans and jammed those in and aggressively chewed.

"I put in full days," I said. "I'm using the alcohol, it's not using me. I want to defend before the summer break."

"Hopefully you're *alive* to defend," he said with his crammed-full mouth.

"Steven, we're simply worried about your health."

"Good for my health is getting this dissertation out of my system."

"What you need is the alcohol out of your system!" said my father.

"We've never seen you like this before," said my mother. "Where did you pick up this habit?"

"In Europe – it's a drinking culture."

"What kind of excuse is that?" said my father taking a swig of his beer.

"Alright then I got it from you."

"From me?!"

"They say alcoholism is a hereditary disease."

"You did *not* get it from me," now slamming down his glass to make the silverware tinkle.

"Well, he didn't get it from me," said my mother in a quieter voice.

"And you're going to drop it this minute!" he said. "So long as you're under my roof! One more drink and you find yourself a hotel, mister!"

"Okay."

"I'm sick of this behavior!"

"I'd like to excuse myself."

"You're excused," said my mother.

So I had to tone things down. It was easily managed by working extra hard in the morning hours then cutting out the alcohol in the afternoon. Also my bedroom had a sliding glass door that opened onto the patio, so now I just put my wine on the ping-pong table and walked out for a slug every paragraph or two, which meant I wasn't drinking "under his roof." I respected him enough that I needed a semi-clear conscience on this count as well as a technical loophole if he somehow discovered I was still hitting the sauce.

2

That winter I drank and wrote and the only things of interest that happened were via post. In February I got delivery of a dozen books from the educational publisher Henshaw-Paul. These were my author's copies of *The Great Gray Masses* which I had edited a year and a half ago for my dissertation adviser Vernon Stewart. It was a two-volume compendium of essays in European cultural history chronicling the lives of non-elites from antiquity to the present. Stewart had done two prior editions but didn't savor revisiting a third and so handed the work off to me. He had given me carte blanche and 40 percent of the royalties, which was generous since the work was for undergraduate courses and had sold quite well as evinced by the third edition, and now I opened the package. On the cover of volumes 1 and 2 were our names in the same size lettering as well as on the spine and title page, while Stewart's preface ended with the words: "In the preparation of this edition I have been aided by the superb editorial skill of Steve McIlhenny, and these volumes have become as much his as mine."

It was like Orson Welles sharing the title card with cameraman Gregg Toland on *Citizen Kane*. Not one professor in a hundred would have done it. Your adviser typically grabbed all the royalties and maybe gave you a reluctant mention in the acknowledgments but otherwise hogged the glory and stuffed you back into oblivion.

And it helped get the parents off my back a little – the kid's doing alright, might make something of himself yet.

Also helping were official job offers from Zafiro Tech and Bonita College. This latter was an expensive private school just a few miles north of Zafiro. The Zafiro contract was limited to the fall quarter and they were merely throwing some teaching experience my way since I was one of their own, but the Bonita contract was for the whole year and contingent on my having the PhD.

Then I got another book in the mail – Stefan Zweig's *Sternstunden der Menschheit* (*Decisive Moments in History*) with an accompanying postcard of Chemnitz, formerly Karl-Marx-Stadt, which featured a montage of the city's sightseeing highlights, among them the glamorous main bus station, and on the back was written in German:

Dear Friend! I traveled with you in the train from Chemnitz to Prague. I wanted to send you the book back then but wasn't able to buy it until now. I wish you much reading pleasure and many good days in your life! Zoltán

This had been on my two-week junket through Eastern Europe the previous spring. For my dissertation research I had already spent a couple months traveling back and forth across the border to East Berlin, not the cheeriest place, so I thought to give the Eastern Bloc another try by seeing Dresden, Prague, Budapest and Bucharest. Zoltán was a Hungarian living with his German wife in Karl-Marx-Stadt, his mother had come for a visit, and he was escorting her back as far as Prague. We fell to talking after mom offered me a hit from her vodka flask, and when Zoltán learned where I was from he told me his dreams of California and how they'd been kindled as a youngster by *Sternstunden der Menschheit*, which had a chapter on Sutter's Mill and the Gold Rush. Did I know it? I didn't. Then I'll send it to you, he said, just give me your address, at which point the door to our compartment slammed open and an unsmiling East German conductor entered. He checked the Hungarians' tickets, exchanged a few words with Zoltán, then took my own ticket and passport in hand.

"U.S.A.?" he said.

"California!" said Zoltán.

The conductor punched my ticket and handed back my passport and turned to Zoltán. "You're not a GDR citizen either."

Zoltán laughed. "And I'm practically the only one who *wants* to live in the GDR!"

Now I opened *Sternstunden der Menschheit*. It had an X inked in the table of contents next to "The Discovery of El Dorado," that certain chapter which had fueled Zoltán's dreams of the Golden State all these years. I'd never been a partisan Californian, no great booster of my native soil, but by the time I returned from two weeks of communism it seemed like El Dorado to me too.

3

In mid-May I finished the dissertation, submitted the 400 pages to my five committee members, and in early June drove down to Zafiro for the defense.

A dissertation defense is as much a formality as the oral exam in advancing to candidacy for the PhD, but the same principle obtains: you don't want to humiliate yourself.

And with Daniel Bardoni on my committee, anything could happen.

Bardoni was the man with whom I'd done my minor-field exam in Renaissance Italy. He wore spectacles and had a pasty complexion and thinning curly black hair and spoke in riddles. He had done his PhD at the "University of Exceptional Brilliance," as we called it, since it was held in special regard by hyperintellectual types and by Bardoni as well, it seemed, since he had this superior puckish grin. The grin wasn't just during conversations with his imagined inferiors but merely as he walked along the campus mall, in his Gilligan hat, like he had some private joke that no one would ever get unless he boasted a doctorate from the University of Exceptional Brilliance. He'd written his dissertation on fourteenth-century Sicilian wheat exports, a quantitative study, but that must have been some youthful indiscretion since Professor Bardoni was the furthest thing imaginable from a number-crunching technocrat and a "just the facts ma'am" approach. In truth he would have turned Sergeant Friday into His Girl Friday, whimpering and pleading for mercy with all the mental loop-de-loops he described. The problem with Bardoni was not so much answering his questions as first deciphering them, and when he wasn't deliberately asking things in a bewildering fashion he was lobbing metaphysical bombs like *Do you buy into the Hegelian notion that ideas ultimately make history?*

That had been courtesy of Bardoni in my oral exam two years before and I was still grappling with the question.

Stewart started things off by throwing down a gardener's glove, as if flinging down the gauntlet, which got some chuckles, then the cross-examination began and was going smoothly, even Bardoni seemed becalmed, until he wasn't. He prefaced his initial query by saying that he found my fact-gathering on the dissertation to be excellent, which coming from Bardoni was an insult, since for him simple knowledge of the facts equated with rote schoolboy learning. Your analytic and above all *interpretive* mettle, regardless how errant, was the mark of a true historian and someone who could mount a successful defense – formality or no – and in clear conscience be awarded the doctorate.

"So the substance of your dissertation would seem to be of solid quality," he continued. "But let's briefly consider your language. For instance in footnote 346 you refer to a duel where the fallen duelist was buried on his wedding day and you write: *Instead of rice they tossed earth.* Now in your view that might be – shall we say – just a tossed-off phrase. But a PhD dissertation has the pretense to being a formal work of scholarship, so we must be careful in our wording, ergo my question to you: Did they in fact toss rice at German weddings in the nineteenth century?"

819 footnotes and THIS one bothered him? I grabbed the gardening glove.

"Well, it does seem as if dueling and gardening go hand in glove."

It fell flat. No chuckles. Not even courtesy ones.

"It might strike you as a trivial point, but there is a wider issue at stake," said Bardoni. "Meaning you may have committed an anachronism – no small matter if we're to lay any claim to professionalism in the writing of history."

The grin.

"I think it safe to assume they threw rice at German weddings," said Stewart impatiently.

"Though it might be interesting to note that rice is a Roman tradition," said the anthropologist whom I'd recruited as one of two committee members you needed from a field not history. "A kind of fertility rite, as I understand it."

"And the Germanic tribes were notoriously resistant to the adoption of Roman mores," Bardoni swooped.

"Which is evidenced in the German language itself," said the second non-history member, an English professor. "The Latin influence is minimal."

"Though in that other German-speaking country I think they threw rice," said the fifth member of my committee, a specialist in Austria. "I remember a passage from Stifter's *Nachsommer* – though it may have been Grillparzer . . ."

This went on for some time, but was the sole glitch in my defense, and if the main thing Bardoni found to criticize was the wording of a single footnote then my dissertation was pretty sound. That evening Stewart and I got tipsy at a fish restaurant overlooking the beach.

"I put your name in for a job opening at the University of Maryland," he said. "I talked you up as the greatest thing since Leopold von Ranke. I don't suppose you've heard from them."

"No."

"Well, be sure to get your placement file in good order now that you have your degree in hand. And you should start revising your dissertation for publication. The quicker you get a book on the market, the better your chances of landing a permanent position."

"Like with Nobleton College Press?"

Stewart had published his dissertation with them.

"That wouldn't hurt."

"What would a press like Nobleton do for me?"

"It would put your name right near the top of short lists."

"You still have a connection there?"

"I'm afraid not, that was a quarter century ago, perish the thought."

We perished more liquor.

"You know," he said, "you're exactly my age when I got my PhD."

"I could have finished it a year earlier if Bardoni hadn't been such a ballbuster for my minor field."

"If you'd completed it a year earlier then you wouldn't have been in Berlin when the Wall came down."

"I wasn't there anyway."

"True enough."

When the waitress came with the check he picked it up as always.

"Thanks Dr. Stewart."

"You can call me Vernon."

"And you can call me Dr. McIlhenny."

"With pleasure."

4

The commencement ceremony was two weeks later. That pretentious hoopla wasn't my bag, but at our dinner Stewart seemed to think it important and had spoken of my presence at the event as a given, so I donned the black gown while he appeared in one of sumptuous red.

"What are you a cardinal?"

"Honor the Crimson, my boy."

I introduced him to my family and they shook hands all around.

"I finally meet the parents of my star student."

"Is he a star?" said my mother. "We had no idea."

"He wears the mantle lightly," said Stewart.

They had over five hundred degrees to award. First came the Master of Arts, then the Master of Fine Arts, then the Master of Pacific International Affairs (a new one on me) then the Master of Science and finally the Doctor of Philosophy. Before they bestowed the degrees they had four separate speakers who broke no new ground in the commencement-speech genre – it was all about us being the bright future and what wonderful opportunities awaited and how life was this great adventure – so I read through the program on my lap. There was some information on our getups, how they were a medieval tradition and had been worn mainly for warmth in unheated buildings by priests and monks who were the first college students, and here we were styling them on the cusp of summer in sun-drenched Zafiro. What you might call an anachronism. My sensitivity to anachronisms had been heightened by Bardoni. I had received a letter from him a few days earlier in which he congratulated me on the dissertation, thought it might be enriched as a book if I versed myself in ethnology, then laid into me again for my language. A couple times in the dissertation I had employed phrases like "the gentle sex" and "the weaker vessel" in referring to women but without quotation marks, which he thought was *tone-deaf sexism*, whereas it was clear to me that I was being tongue-in-cheek. It was the way German duelists saw their womenfolk whose delicate honor needed protection in a duel, in fact my entire thesis was a critical reading of this certain male ritual, and I wrote Bardoni back a letter where I politely but firmly rejected his allegation. Stewart had me make a copy of our exchange because he felt the accusation of sexism could potentially hurt me and by extension him. He hoped the matter would rest there, but if not then it was best to be armed and ready. So this was the world I was presently inhabiting and preparing to navigate careerwise, ah yes, the great adventure lay ahead . . .

"And now for award of the degree of Doctor of Philosophy!"

We got in line. They weren't playing *Pomp and Circumstance* – instead a string trio did something less grandiose and hence more seemly. My graduation ceremonies for high school, college and the Masters degree had made a big deal of the thing, but it was just meatheads being churned through the system.

Me included. Yet now I felt the fanfare commensurate. The doctorate itself was no wondrous feat but I had done it on my own terms, at speed, and there were enough Asians in line right now for me to feel somewhat brainy.

"Steven McIlhenny – hooded by Dr. Vernon Stewart!"

My family clapped.

I mounted the stage and Stewart stood there looking like Richelieu. I handed him the hood and turned toward the audience. He couldn't get it down past one corner of my cap, I removed the cap, and he slipped the hood round my neck and let it dangle in back like the slack of a noose. I turned and we shook hands. Then I shook hands with a woman who was some deputy assistant vice provost, then with the Dean of Graduate Studies, then I replaced my mortarboard and left the stage and returned to my seat and was part of the club.

Outside we took pictures. Me with the family, me with Stewart, me standing alone on my newly conferred dignity. Then I went out on the surrounding grass and mimicked Myron's *Discus Thrower* with my mortarboard as discus. They snapped the picture and I did a follow-through and flipped the mortarboard in the air and caught it and walked back.

"Always adding your own little touch, aren't you?" said Stewart.

"That's what made me your star student."

"Don't get cocky now," said my mother.

"Now?" said my father.

I received my official sheepskin in the mail a couple

weeks later. It had the golden seal and facsimile signatures and "all the rights and privileges thereto pertaining." I was curious as to what exactly those rights and privileges might entail, but wasn't getting my hopes too high.

5

In September I was back at Zafiro teaching the upper-division course "Europe 1870-1945" and at Bonita College teaching "World Civ 1" and "World Civ 2" as well as the upper-division course "Germany 1870-1945." That meant a total of ten lectures a week, which meant not only giving but preparing them. I had never taught these courses before and couldn't fall back on old lecture notes, so had to whip up notes from scratch each time, not to mention dividing myself between two campuses, two administrative systems, holding office hours and grading umpteen papers along with mid-terms and final exams. I was accorded a grader for the Zafiro course, which had sixty students, but that was like sticking your finger in one solitary hole of a dyke which was spraying leaks all up and down its length.

The Europe and Germany courses I had pretty much under control; I could fake "World Civ 2" since it was mostly Europe from 1300 onward; but "World Civ 1" was shakier terrain (Sumerian Revival, Achaean League, Code of Justinian) so I took the line of least resistance and just copied lectures out of my old world-history textbook from high school. It was a decent book, presenting the material in a categorical and lucid fashion – in fact I should have given my students *this* book – but then they would have just read the thing with no need for a lecture-course and they themselves now privy to what qualified me as "Professor." Their official class book was one of those overly detailed and PC jobs that was all over the map both literally and figuratively, which played right into my hands, for now I with my Spenglerian vision and out-of-print textbook would bestow clarity, synthesis and enlightenment.

Like the time I was going through the Ten Commandments and got the fifth mixed up with the sixth – stealing instead of killing, I think it was, though I still haven't gotten them straight. Or when I bestowed the name "Augustus" on Octavian in the period before he became emperor, the Roman Senate seeing fit to bestow that honorific only after his accession to power. Or the lecture where I made passing reference to those two monumental pyramids of Egypt's Old Kingdom: Cheops and Khufu. They're the same pyramid, in case you didn't know, Cheops just the Greek name for Khufu. A student called me on it and I could only make a clean breast and admit I'd screwed up – as I'd also been forced to admit with the Ten Commandments and Octavian and any number of other gaffes.

How's that for instilling faith in your intellectual authority?

These little missteps might have seemed excusable in light of how busy I was shuffling lecture notes, but the kids didn't know how harassed I was and wouldn't have cared even had they known.

I always held office hours right before class. No one ever came. They probably thought I was a charlatan and were right. So I got in the habit of using those 45 minutes to finish plagiarizing my lecture. It was a hassle, I wished I could have just made xerox copies and gone through them with a highlighter, but you had to use handwritten notes or else they'd be on to you. O wearisome toil! Today I was holding forth on Confucianism and ancient Chinese civilization, both of which I knew reams of nothing about.

A knock at the door.

I covered the high-school textbook with my yellow legal pad.

"Come in."

It was Scheherazade. She was majoring in international relations, daughter of an Egyptian diplomat, and of course she'd been the one to catch my pyramid mistake. She took a chair and sat there wrinkling her forehead.

"Dr. McIlhenny, what's the *theme* of our course?"

"The theme?"

"I mean like with a novel. You're reading it and your friend asks what it's about and even if you're only halfway through you can tell her. We're already halfway through this course and that's what I need to know: What's this course *about*?"

"Mankind's ascent to civilization."

"You mean some civilizations were higher than others?"

"Not higher – just more advanced."

"What's the difference? And isn't that a value-judgment? Didn't Greek civilization get anything from the Egyptians?"

"They got their astronomy from the Egyptians," hoping it wasn't the Babylonians.

"And the rest was the Greeks' own creation?"

"You might say that."

"And might you say that it's the people who make the great civilization or the great civilization that makes the people?"

"I don't think I'm saying either."

"But what *would* you say?"

"I'd say that geographical conditions help create a culture and the culture creates a type."

Throw her off by ditching the word civilization.

"And what do you mean by geographical conditions – that they all had their start next to rivers?"

That was one of the axioms I had regurgitated from my high-school textbook.

"Sure – just look what emerged along the Indus, the Nile, the Tigris and Euphrates. You need settled communities and a crop surplus to free people up to be artisans and architects and forge an urban nexus."

"But Greece didn't have a river."

"Athens did," I said. "A small one."

"What was its name?"

"It evades me at the moment."

"And you're from Los Angeles – that's a major urban center and there's no big river there."

"We import our water."

Water was the last thing I was drinking. After my classes I would drive to one of several liquor stores, rotating them so the proprietors wouldn't think I was the full-blown souse I was in danger of becoming. I tested various brands and finally hit on Canadian Velvet whisky. I bought the flask bottle, a pint or so, and the blend was so agreeable that after a while I didn't care what any given storeowner might think and just headed to this little place owned by a Chinese guy who always had it in stock even with my daily purchases. Right across the street from his store was a gas station where I tanked up, a couple doors down was a good Mexican eatery, so in that one small triangle I had my food, fuel and firewater. With my farcical work situation just up the hill. A homey arrangement if you weren't ambitious. Then I returned to my apartment and propped myself in bed and cracked the bottle. It went down smoothly, that mahogany elixir, and after a couple stiff shots I got out my textbooks and grad-school notes and yellow foolscap and prepared my lectures for the next day. There was no way I could start scribbling before I had taken one or two hits, I first had to wash my mind of the previous gunk, but if I waited much past the second drink then it required too much effort to apply myself to the task at hand, so I was always very careful.

This was medicine, not a good time.

I wasn't intoxicated with my subject matter – just intoxicated – but I only had to suck it up till Christmas break because the World Civ 1 & 2 courses that I would give again in spring were of course being composed this fall, and for the spring upper-division course "Europe 1815-1914" there would be just two new preparations each week. Several guys from the Zafiro course "Europe 1870-1945" wanted me for a directed reading in Nazi Germany that coming spring as well (we got the administration to approve it) but that would be minimal preparation since I knew the Nazi stuff cold, so all this sozzled note-taking was an investment and I toughed it out, as did my students, who probably liked me in the end since I was guilty of grade inflation that whole semester. Final grades for "World Civ 1" were eighteen *A*'s, twenty-one *B*'s, eight *C*'s and no *D*'s or *F*'s, though some quite richly deserved, but I'd plainly not gotten the material across, it wasn't the kids' fault, so I cut them slack. Didactic incompetence bred grade inflation! This was my great insight that fall. And because grade inflation was such a chronic problem at American universities, there had to be massive incompetence out there, which made me feel better about my own piss-poor pedagogy, for about two minutes, then I got my teaching evaluations from the students:

The material covered in this course was nothing more than what I learned in high school history classes.

I have often wondered if he knows what he's talking about. The lectures just seemed a collection of other people's lectures and words.

He did not seem to fully understand what he was lecturing on. Most of the time, some of the students knew about the material more than he did. And he should get a nicer duffel bag – the red and gold one doesn't cut it.

The instructor began the course in a state of confusion. The ideas that he focused on seemed to be the minor ideas, while the major concepts were breezed over. He spent a whole class telling how Napoleon lost Waterloo because of hemorrhoids, like he could have won it hemorrhoid-free.

You kind of have to give the guy, Prof. McIlhenny, a break because he is new to the job. But my Grandma, who died 3 yrs ago, could give a more exciting and insightful lecture.

6

Modern Continental European Intellectual and Cultural.
*The history department at _____ University invites
applications for a tenure-eligible assistant professorship
to begin September 1991 contingent upon budgetary approval. Research specialization in 19th or 20th-century
German-speaking Europe is particularly desired, but
applications from all areas of continental Europe from
the early 18th century onward are welcomed and encouraged. Applicants will be expected to participate in
teaching Western political thought within the history
component of the Directed Studies Program during
the term of their appointment, with preference for a
specialist in women's history and the ability to teach
some Third World history. Completion and successful
defense of the PhD dissertation before September 1, 1991
required. Terms of appointment for assistant professorships are ordinarily five years with possible promotion
to the rank of associate and beyond. Starting salaries
are tied to a fixed scale. Applicants should send letter of
application, curriculum vitae, official transcripts, a summary of no more than five pages of their dissertation or
other current research, an article-length writing sample,
and at least three current letters of recommendation to
Prof. Stanley Pedanski, Chair, Search Committee, Dept.
of History, _____ University, PO Box 12345,
_____ . Priority will be given to applications
received before December 1, 1990.*

*

Dear Dr. McIlhenny:

Thank you for your response to our recent employment announcement for the position in Modern European History. Your résumé and other materials have been received and will be reviewed by the Search Committee.

As you are no doubt aware, selecting a new member of our faculty is a very thorough and time-consuming process involving a number of individuals. For your information, the pre-campus interview segment of a search typically includes the following phases:

Phase 1 – Search Committee members review all materials and select candidates for preliminary interview at the National Alliance of Historians convention.

Phase 2 – Invited candidates interviewed at NAH convention in New York (December 1990).

Phase 3 – Semifinalists are asked to submit written interviews that are evaluated by the Search Committee.

Phase 4 – Finalists are selected and invited to campus for personal interviews.

If after your materials are reviewed and we find that your credentials and experience are appropriate to our needs, we will contact you concerning an interview at the NAH convention by December 10, 1990.

*

Dear Dr. McIlhenny:

My colleagues and I look forward to meeting you at the NAH convention in New York. We will have 20 minutes to answer your questions about the position and to ask a few questions about your teaching and research interests. Your interview time is _____ in room _____ .

*

I got five other letters just like it, which meant six interviews total, all taking place in the Hilton Hotel where the convention was being held. When I arrived at the registration desk it was crowded with cleancut men in business suits and self-assured women in pantsuits and all of them with their name-and-institutional-affiliation tags pinned to their lapels. I felt like a phony jerk in my own newly purchased outfit and toting a black briefcase on loan from my father for the occasion, which was nice of him since it contained my updated CV – a bottle of Canadian Velvet. I picked up my name-tag then checked the bulletin board on the off chance that there might be messages for me, and there were, from a couple universities that needed one-year and two-year replacements, respectively, and telling me the time and place we could meet tomorrow. So eight interviews. I pocketed the notes and took the elevator to where my first college was holding court and knocked on the door.

"Gimme a couple minutes!"

I moved off from the door and waited for five. A man emerged and we eyeballed each other as he went past. A fellow jobseeker. I waited for the door to open again and have the interviewer greet me, but that didn't happen, so I called down the corridor after the guy: "Did you just come from an interview?"

"It's my room!"

"Who'd you think I was?"

"The maid!"

My brain needed a maid. I was more jittery than I thought. I went back down to the registration desk, found the correct room number, quickly consulted my CV, then hurried back up.

Their trio sat on the bed while I took my place in a chair in the corner. The ringleader was a guy with darting eyes and a mustache that didn't belong on his little-boy face. His technique was to make smart remarks and see if you could top them, if you couldn't then he pursued his next line of questioning until it gave him another chance to crack wise, he gave you a millisecond to reply in kind and, if not, then on to something else.

After fifteen minutes I left baffled by the whole thing.

The next interview was conducted by a priest and a woman professor. Despite my blundering answer on how I might arrange a senior honors seminar around the theme of post-1945 Europe, the two of them were soothing and agreeable and we got on famously. The priest wore a long black cassock and was one of those older, red-faced, alcoholic Jesuits who has tenure the day he assumes holy orders and doesn't take these things too seriously, if at all, the world his wine-filled chalice, so he hung back and let the woman run the show. She had voluminous breasts and was very earnest, one of those people who never misspeaks and whom you can always rely on to say the judicious thing. *Yes, I couldn't agree with you more, Dr. McIlhenny, you are so right, **absolutely** right.* One guy who had interviewed with them told me later that he'd had a similar good experience with the woman, the candidate they interviewed before me had left the hotel room with an ear-to-ear grin as though she'd also had a splendid interaction, and I was sure that the airport check-in girl and the door-to-door pollster had equally pleasant encounters with what was now my own nominee for NAH's Miss Congeniality Award 1990.

Then some excitement kicked in.

It was four professors examining me, though de facto three. The fourth guy sat to my right in an easychair and never opened his mouth, just wore an amused smirk, as well he might have. Leading the interview was a man named Seegelbaum, then another older Jewish guy, and finally a former undergrad student of Stewart's who announced this fact up front and which fooled me into thinking that she might be kindly disposed toward her erstwhile professor's doctoral charge. I gave a brief rundown of my dissertation and she asked what research methodology I had employed.

"None in particular," I said. "Just scoured the archives to see what turned up."

"You proceeded willy-nilly? But you must have had a theoretical template, some kind of working hypothesis."

"Well, it may sound flippant but I followed my gut, that's all the template I need."

I wanted to quash that subject and quick. I'd had this type of exchange before. You got tangled up in a discussion about structuralism and critical theory and who knows what else, so I thought it shrewder to run the risk of being judged an arrogant jackass rather than a clueless bullshit artist.

"Your gut," she said. "Not your brain? Not your analytic faculty?"

"I'm sure Dr. McIlhenny means his visceral sense as *informed* by his analytic faculty," said Seegelbaum.

"But perhaps we should make a distinction between your research methods and your methodology per se," she pursued. "In reading the abstract of your dissertation, it would seem that you're doing a thick description of the German duel à la Clifford Geertz, a multi-level analysis of its symbolic properties, while also applying Pierre Bourdieu's notion of cultural capital – would that be a fair rendering?"

I thought it a fairly pompous rendering.

"I'm placing the duel in its cultural context," I said. "If that's what you mean."

"So a phenomenological approach. Yet we hear this phrase quite a bit – cultural context – and I'm wondering what you might understand by it."

"You want my definition?"

"I want you to break it down for me. First off, what do you understand by *culture*."

The smirker was lapping it up.

"A society's self-conception," I said. "The shared

beliefs in people's heads. And to get into their heads at a collective level you don't just look at their artifacts or listen to their words but examine their rituals. That's where the rubber meets the road. And I'd say risking your life in a duel was one of German society's less frivolous rituals."

"And context?"

"The same words or actions can express different things," now drawing on that ethnology prescribed by Bardoni. "The German duel had similar protocol to the French duel but a wholly different meaning. It expressed caste-consciousness while the French duel evoked democratic values. You tease out those differences by looking at the surrounding societies."

"So you've adopted a socio-comparative approach at the nation-state level."

"Yeah."

Which made her happy. She wanted to affix fancy lingo to what for me was common sense. She had successfully promoted my little tale of German dueling to a comparative phenomenological study employing multi-level strategies adapted from cultural anthropology.

Tenure for her was just a matter of time.

"Let's talk courses," said Seegelbaum. "I see you gave a class on modern Germany this fall and will be supervising a graduate directed reading in Nazi Germany this spring. It seems you're deeply invested in the field. Are there any other courses you could imagine giving which might be subsumed under the German history rubric?"

I proposed a couple other courses.

"And you're not gonna give a course on Hitler?" piped up the older Jewish guy.

"Specifically Hitler?" I said. "I could teach a course on Hitler, sure, no problem."

"And how much time would you give to a discussion of the Holocaust?"

"I'd devote an entire lecture to it."

"Just one? A single lecture? We're talking *Hitler* here, whose whole ideology culminated in destruction of the Jews."

"How about two."

"How about a complete course – seeing as how the Holocaust is the central and defining event of the twentieth century."

I told him I could do a complete course.

"And what would your guiding idea be," he said. "That Hitler killed the Jews or the Germans did?"

"They needed each other, neither of them alone could have done it."

"So that's your viewpoint."

"Yes."

"How about the viewpoint of a Jew in an Auschwitz oven?"

"I'm afraid I can't speak on his behalf."

Seegelbaum stepped in, successfully diverting the conversation, then the interview wound down and I left the Hilton and trudged carefully in my smooth-bottomed dress shoes over the hard-packed snow to my cheaper digs some blocks away.

7

The following day my first interview was with a small liberal arts college in Georgia. The two guys conducting it struck me as a bit redneck, and had they offered me the job on the spot then I would have said no. My next interview was with another Southern college and early on it became clear that I wasn't right for the job, we all knew it, yet went through the motions like you always do and at interview's end I recommended a colleague of mine whom they had also interviewed for the position. It cost me nothing. Then the two interviews for the replacement jobs were very pro forma and not at all memorable.

My last interview was memorable. This didn't take place in a hotel room but in one of the Hilton's conference rooms where I faced *six* blue suits. Smooth-shaven, short hair parted on the side, poker-faced, corporate. Like an interview with Proctor & Gamble. No wonder they'd picked a conference room. We sat at an oblong table with glossy wood veneer, their massed erudition on one side and me on the other, but I'd gotten lots of rehearsal by this stage so gave solid practiced replies. Yet I was performing with too much authority, too much aplomb, thus had to be taken down and again it was a woman. Didn't I mention her? I was keeping her as a surprise. She was one of the blue suits too, wearing a blue skirt and blue jacket over a white blouse and at her throat a droopy red bowtie. The stewardess uniform, and not unbefitting, as she was stunning and statuesque, even sitting down, with sheeny brown hair past her shoulders, not ruthlessly cropped like most of the battleaxes you found on history faculties. Her looks were showy enough that I thought to have seen her recently in the monthly newsletter of the *NAH Quarterly*. She had won a financial award from some research foundation, which included a trip to Washington D.C. and a check for 500 dollars, and in the photo she held the outsize cardboard check while wearing an outsize smile like she'd won millions in the lottery. This was a penurious trade but the smile was way too big for just half a grand. I didn't trust it. Toward end of the interview she gleamed that 500-dollar smile and laid into me.

"Dr. McIlhenny, while you were speaking of your dissertation I made note of the fact that you use the term caste-consciousness and not *class*-consciousness in describing the reason why the upper orders dueled."

"Caste-consciousness was one of the reasons."

"But presumably caste-consciousness is your rendition of Marx's class-consciousness, with which he sought to imbue the proletariat for the very reason that class-consciousness wasn't truly present in a substantial way back then, and hence my question to you: Did the term caste-consciousness actually *exist* in Imperial Germany? And if not, if the phrase is indeed one of your own coinage, are you not then guilty of an anachronism? Not to put too fine a point on it, but was it even *possible* for your German duelists to be caste-conscious devoid of some normative linguistic expression of that conceptual mindset?"

I finally realized what was screwy about academics: they didn't write like they talked but talked like they wrote. Apart from that, I wasn't even sure the bit about Marx was true, though very likely true was that this woman had studied at the University of Exceptional Brilliance (I later checked her credentials – she'd done her undergraduate work there) and it was just unlucky for her that I'd already been given the UEB treatment and knew how to handle myself.

"They were certainly conscious of their caste," I replied, "so they logically had caste-consciousness, but they didn't go around using the *term* caste-consciousness so probably weren't all that *conscious* of being caste-conscious."

"So what term, if any, did duelists use in describing why they dueled?"

"Their term was *Standesehre*, which translates as caste-honor, another reason I assume they had caste-consciousness."

"But if they called it caste-*honor* then why not simply retain their own language?"

"Well, to paraphrase Mae West, honor had nothing to do with it."

Her smile wasn't so winning this time, barely tolerating the joke, while one of the blue suits gave an amused snort.

"And returning to your original question," I said, "as to why caste-consciousness instead of *class*-consciousness – class imputes an economic rationale. Dueling made little sense from an economic standpoint, it had more to do with a militarized society and anachronistic notions of reprisal."

If she wanted to talk anachronisms.

"So you're obviously not applying Marx here."

"I wouldn't apply Marx anywhere."

"That's a rather blanket statement."

"Not blanket enough," I said. "I'm actually anti-Marx."

I didn't quite hear a collective gasp from the blue suits, but their complete silence was the next best thing. Like most history faculties, you just knew that half of them were armchair Marxists and the other half didn't have the balls to be outspoken opponents.

"Would you care to explain?" her smile now brightening, like she couldn't wait to see me dig my way out of this one.

"Marxism is a dismal system," I replied. "It deadens the human spirit and turns people into whipped dogs. Were you ever in Romania under Ceauşescu?"

"No – but presumably you were."

"Yes. It's a gray and joyless place. He ruined Bucharest – the Paris of the Balkans is now more like Detroit. I was also in Berlin when the Wall came down. I've never seen happier people than those pouring across the border. In five minutes I saw more smiles on those East Berlin faces than I had in two months of basically living there."

"You seem to know quite a bit about the subject."

I explained about knowing quite a bit – while leaving out my Rip Van Winkle moment.

"As the product of an unapologetically capitalist system, you can't have gone in with a neutral posture," said one of the five guys who probably had the hots for the girl and was trying to appear chivalrous by making a conspicuous show of deflecting my impertinence his way. "It can't be said that you were some pristine tabula rasa."

"Of course not," I said. "And would you look at Nazism from a neutral posture?"

"Are you drawing a moral equivalence between Nazis and communism?"

"Not really. I rate communism the greater evil. It's killed a lot more people and lasted decades longer."

That effectively ended our interview not to mention my chances. But I was still sore about the Holocaust guy from the day before – and this one was for Zoltán and his mom and the other big-hearted people I'd met behind the Iron Curtain.

*

Next day at the airport I saw Joe Vasquez. He was an Iberianist from Zafiro who was what we called ABD – "All But Dissertation" – meaning he'd passed his oral examination but hadn't yet completed his doctoral thesis. Joe was one of those few in the department with whom I had any rapport, and I told him about my interviews.

"You can't forget the Holy Trinity of race, class and gender," he said. "And race always trumps the other two."

"You know, Joe, I don't think in those categories."

"What categories do you think in?"

"Courage, beauty and right action."

*

Dear Dr. McIlhenny:

I regret to inform you that we have decided not to pursue your candidacy for our position in modern European history. We have narrowed our search to three candidates who more closely suit our needs. Given the fact that we had more than 160 applications, our decision should in no way be construed as a reflection on the quality of your credentials.

Thanks so much for your interest in _____ University and please accept our warmest wishes for success and satisfaction in your future professional endeavors.

*

I received seven other letters just like it.

8

That spring semester I wasn't so harried. At Zafiro I had only the directed reading in Nazi Germany, at Bonita the two world-history courses were now nailed down, and it was just twice a week that I had to prepare a 75-minute lecture for "Europe 1815-1914," which was right in my wheelhouse. There was room to breathe and I took the first steps toward revising my dissertation for publication. I had already made contact with a guy who was writing on the French duel and had published his previous book with Noble-ton College Press, he recommended my dissertation to the history editor there, she requested sample chapters which I sent and her interest didn't wane, so now I was making a concerted effort to get the thing in shape.

I'd never been to Israel, it had never occurred to me to go there, but at Stewart's prompting I applied for and got a postdoc at Yalom Eldad University – or more precisely their INSTITUTE FOR WOMEN'S STUDIES AND FEMALE EMPOWERMENT. The topic of their coming six-month seminar was **Women in Late-Modern Europe: The Socio-Cultural Other in Imaging Gender**. I wormed my way into that one since a chapter of my dissertation was "Women and the Duel" – which apparently qualified me to now enter the man-eating jaws of academic feminism. Just reading the list of papers scheduled for the seminar made me jumpy. All of them had "Gender" or "Other" or both in the title, so I threw something really deviant their way: *Female Honor and Male Chivalry in Imperial Germany.*

Let them puzzle over that one for a while.

There were seventeen women and just three guys including myself in the seminar. I had heard flattering things about Israeli women, who comprised most of the participants, and at very least I might get a good *Penthouse* forum piece out of it. *I am here on a postdoc at Yalom Eldad University, in a seminar on women's history, and the women-to-men ratio is five to one* . . . In any case I saw the fellowship as a deft riposte to Bardoni's accusation of "tone-deaf sexism." After my abortive NAH convention he extended an offer to meet and discuss my future prospects, and it was over lunch that I told him about Israel.

"Did you take my advice about the sexist language?"

"I'm afraid not."

"Then congratulations are doubly in order."

We were sitting in the Gramsci Grotto. It was a wood shack covered with murals of radical leftists like V. I. Lenin and Angela Davis and of course the café's Italian Marxist namesake. In order to avoid any political hassles that might preclude their getting university subsidies, the letters GRAMSCI had been formally registered with the Zafiro administration as an acronym for "**GR**eat **AM**erican **S**nack & **C**offee **I**nitiative," and the sign above the shack read: *Gramsci Grotto – Student Organization Offices.* I had no clue what they were organizing. Likely civil unrest. I told Bardoni about New York.

"It seems your class is really up against it," he said. "I chaired a medieval history search this fall. We had over a hundred applicants and four-fifths were recent PhDs from last year."

"Who did you finally hire?"

"We canceled the search for lack of funding."

"So you think I have a shot at anything?"

"Oh certainly – I see you at a good state school."

This was another of Bardoni's veiled barbs. But I was so used to them that I didn't take offense and at this stage was even grateful he had taken the trouble to say "good." We parted with him recommending that I change the title of my dissertation, which was *The Last Imperial Knights* and which he felt was a trope and I could do better. After lunch I continued on straight to the main library and looked up the word "trope" to see if its technical definition was as bad as I assumed it was coming from Bardoni . . .

9

On the approach to Ben Gurion Airport my plane full of Israelis started singing *Hava Nagila*. I joined in the rhythmic clapping – relieved as always to be arriving safely – but also getting my feet wet in this first stage of the acculturation process. Just like Berlin, a full submersion, ready to go native! I slogged through security and customs and caught a taxi for my hotel where I unpacked then went and found a restaurant. I took my seat and a beautiful mocha-skinned girl with emerald eyes and raven hair down her back came for my order. I would come to recognize this brand of Israeli, sometimes they had sapphire eyes, but whatever color they were Yemenite girls. I ordered humus with pita bread and a beer.

"Maccabee or Goldstar?"

"Huh?"

"Your beer," she said. "Maccabee or Goldstar."

"Goldstar."

The humus filled an entire plate and had a pool of olive oil in the middle. The pita bread was hot and came in a basket. I tore the bread in strips and dragged them through the humus. The beer was good too and I ordered another half liter.

"A second one?" said the waitress with a look on her face like she might have to call me a cab.

"Yeah, another Goldberg."

"Goldstar."

Maybe trying to acculturate a bit too hard.

Next day I took a bus to the university for the first meeting of our seminar. Heading it was Miriam Florsheim who also ran the INSTITUTE FOR WOMEN'S STUDIES AND FEMALE EMPOWERMENT. She was a handsome lady of fifty with arched eyebrows and almond-shaped eyes behind round glasses, and those eyes really *looked* at you, sizing you up and taking you in and filing you away in her more-than-capacious brain for future reference. If you were lucky. She seemed like the right choice to direct an institute for female power. As I'd been apprised, the seminar was all women except for an Israeli guy and another American who was an assistant professor of Jewish Studies. After the meeting I asked if he wanted to room together and save money since the rents in Yalom Eldad were reputedly steep.

"Love to," he said. "Though we'll still be paying up the wazoo for anything short of a Mossad torture-room reject."

Jeremy was his name and his vote of confidence endearing – though he was probably just used to living with someone since he was married and his wife presently back in the States. We found an apartment in a northern suburb of Yalom Eldad, fifteen minutes by bus to the seminar in the Frankelhirsch Library, whose holdings were devoted to the Third Reich and the Holocaust. They had a big map of the death camps on the wall and beneath it was a glass case with caricatures from the Nazi anti-Jewish rag *Der Stürmer*. A majority of seminar participants had individual offices in the Frankelhirsch, while Jeremy and I were consigned to a big glassed-in area with wooden cubicles, some equipped with machines for viewing microfilm. Jeremy had an early laptop and I used a clunky PC and dot-matrix printer that were installed for me by the Frankelhirsch librarians, whom we got to know and like, and they let us roam the archives in back and examine things like the original *Protocols of the Elders of Zion*. In its holdings the Frankelhirsch had not only documents but objects, such as antisemitic games for kids, and Jeremy and I gave two or three a whirl. One was a ring-toss with cardboard cutouts of caricatured Jews like in *Der Stürmer*. The caricatures had number values assigned to them and you put the cutouts on little stands and stood back and tried to accumulate points. There were also boardgames like "Der Siegeslauf des Haken-kreuzes" ("Triumphal March of the Swastika") where you trod the historical path of the Nazi party's progress from its founding through to the failed Beer Hall Putsch – go back three spaces! – to the 1930 Reichstag elections – advance five spaces! – to Hitler's final power grab. Another game was "Juden raus!" ("Jews Out!") where each player moved a figurine around the board and gathered up conical tokens with supposedly Jewish faces drawn on them and stacked these on the figurine like little dunce caps. You amassed the tokens by rolling dice then bringing them to collection points outside the city where they would be deported to Palestine. The aim was to deport half a dozen Jews, which you were enjoined to do by a catchy slogan emblazoned across the middle of the board: "Gelingt es dir, 6 Juden rauszujagen, so bist du Sieger, ohne zu fragen!"

Succeed in chasing 6 Jews out, you're the winner without a doubt!

Cute.

By the time we'd had four or five colloquia, I was already suffering mental fatigue. It was always the same thing – women as the marginalized and oppressed "Other" and the male patriarchy as archnemesis. They never threw you a curveball like *women* kicking ass and sticking it to *men*. I could cite a whole slew of such instances with yours truly as downtrodden victim, so there had to be larger historical examples, but instead it was all about the trauma women had endured at the hands of my own tyrannical sex – which they could pillory all they liked, I didn't take it personally, but it was so damn uniform and *predictable.*

I had read enough history to know that it was never uniform and rarely predictable.

Miriam seemed as unimpressed as me. But since she was skippering this ship of galley slaves to feminist theory and grievance politics, their oars in perfect sync, she let them row their little hearts out and in our sessions generally restricted herself to a cogent summary at the end of each talk while attempting to salvage some intellectual takeaway, howsoever scant. Jeremy and I always sat together, trying to restrain ourselves, but sometimes they just made it impossible. An otherwise attractive Israeli woman, a self-defined "post-feminist/post-structuralist," was giving a paper with the title: *Toward Reclaiming the Feminine Sphere: Department-Store Shopping in Late Nineteenth-Century Bratislava.* She droned on: "The department store was a female cultural space, a domain where the modern urban male would feel as disenfranchised from his environment as women had always felt in the patriarchy at large, a kind of performative revenge enacted by females on their gender-privileged counterparts . . ."

"Not unlike the Frankelhirsch seminar," Jeremy whispered.

". . . a place where women could reclaim female agency and achieve true selfhood while being unafraid to pose naive and even outwardly stupid questions . . ."

"Not unlike the Frankelhirsch seminar," I whispered back.

She finally finished and our discussion kicked off.

"I want to first extend a word of thanks for your superb presentation," came one woman's unfailing statement of solidarity. "And I think I speak for all present in expressing my admiration for the tremendous *courage* it requires to take on such a controversial and emotionally fraught topic. Your reframing of the narrative seems to come from a place of authentic concern not only for female empowerment but transgressive Otherness in a world of hegemonic masculinity."

"Thank you, that was indeed the subtext informing my work. I seek to shed new light on women's self-construction as they subvert and dismantle the gender binary. Following Kristeva, I wish to introduce this narrative into the post-feminist discourse so as to ascertain precisely where women inhabit their real and potential space . . ."

After the seminar Jeremy and I walked down the stairs together.

"You know," he said, "I've finally figured out what this seminar's all about."

"A cheerleading squad for Team Woman."

"Not really, deep-down it's group therapy."

Bullseye.

10

The next session was someone I had grown to deplore. It might sound like I had grown to deplore the whole seminar, but some of the individual participants were okay. Most of these women weren't aggressive man-haters so much as deluded and pathetic. I had friendly relations with the majority in an ironically amused way – since God knows what they were thinking of *me* – but Amity Susskind was a different animal. She was a chubby late-modern Europeanist, just two years out of an Ivy League PhD program, who went around loudly condemning President George Bush and threatening to turn her back on the United States and leave it permanently if the Republicans took the White House in '92 for the fourth time running since women and minorities had suffered *egregiously* at their crypto-fascist hands. Maybe I should have told Amity that I was a registered Democrat, though it likely wouldn't have helped, as she had taken an instant dislike to me – in contrast to the others who may not have cared for my person but this only after repeated exposure. Amity loathed me on sight. I likely embodied what she had devoted her whole career to combating: the cocksure, unrepentant male oppressor. Not that I styled myself this way. But I knew I probably gave off those vibes to someone of her ilk, and no use trying to endear myself since that wouldn't have fit her theory, and theory was her lifeblood since it nurtured the career which defined her existence. A career-woman, Dr. Amity Susskind, no husband or children of course, probably a lesbian though I wasn't sure, more than likely neuter, so I wished to sustain her life's meaning and purpose by confirming all her long-held beliefs – nay certainties! – regarding the unapologetic rogue male. Each time I opened my mouth in the seminar, which was seldom, I hoped it would irk Amity, and of course Jeremy was on board with all this.

"I think you really got to her today."

"How could you tell?"

"If foam at the mouth is any indicator, you got to her."

"But how many i.e.'s?"

"I only counted three."

Among her other winning qualities, Amity had a habit of rattling along in fluent albeit jargon-ridden English but then bringing things to a screeching halt by incorporating this certain device used chiefly in expository prose: *I think you have a fine project, it's positively bristling with potential, yet in my humble view you'll need to revisit the archives, i.e. dig deeper into the original source-material . . .* At least one "i.e." snuck in every time she held forth and it was a game to see how many she would perpetrate during the two hours of our seminar – but this no more than just an ancillary pastime to our more wide-ranging project of simply how to PISS OFF AMITY. Jeremy was worse than me in some ways since he liked playing the Jewish card. He did this with others as well. One day two German girls from our seminar were standing at the glass case with the *Stürmer* caricatures when Jeremy and I walked past on our way to lunch.

"Horrible," said Jeremy. "Don't you think?"

They mouthed the usual platitudes, showing proper German remorse and contrition.

"But pretty accurate," he declared. "I see guys like this in the old city in Jerusalem all the time."

We continued to lunch with dead silence at our backs.

Another day Amity Susskind entered our cubicle. She gave us a cool nod, sat down with some microfilm and began scanning it through the machine. Jeremy stretched out his arms and sighed.

"Hey Steve, I don't know about you, but I could use a good game of *Juden raus* about now."

"Great minds think alike."

Jeremy rapped on the window to grab Nirit's attention. "Nirit – *Juden raus!*"

Nirit was a hefty babe of Polish extraction and always right on the ball with our requests – whether of a scholarly, administrative or purely whimsical nature. She wasn't some stepinfetchit, she was mistress of all she surveyed and did things solely at her pleasure, but she had sort of adopted us, which was good since she was strong as hell and could have clobbered both of us sequentially. She was also an ace when it came to solving computer glitches or fixing just whatever needed repair – the best advertisement I've ever seen for growing up on a kibbutz – and of course someone like her wasn't going to candy to the Amity Susskinds of the world.

"Per your request, gentlemen, have fun," said Nirit as

she came bustling in with the game, then on her way out, as a kind of afterthought: "Oh, hi Amity."

We set up the board, began rolling dice and rounding up Jews.

"Could you please keep it down," said Amity turning from her microfilm.

We apologized. She readdressed the microfilm, we readdressed the game, but our decibel level didn't reduce to her satisfaction.

"You know you're making it *impossible* to work," she said. "And what *is* it you're playing?"

"Parcheesi with a twist," said Jeremy.

"And what might that twist be? Overexuberant cacophony?"

"You don't want to know," I said.

"At this point I think it's my right to know."

Jeremy recited the game's slogan, but like most francophone historians, Amity's German was zilch.

"Translation please?"

Jeremy translated and I enlarged upon the rules.

"That's abhorrent," she said. "It's a hate game, it propagates antisemitism."

"We're reframing that narrative," said Jeremy. "Come over and grab a figure."

"Count me out. But the folks at Hamas might be interested, i.e. licking their collective chops."

"I doubt it," I said. "This is about sending Jews to Palestine."

"It's still a Nazi game."

"Actually no," said Jeremy. "The Nazis distanced themselves from it. They thought it trivialized their noble effort to rid the Fatherland of the Jewish pathogen."

Amity distanced herself from us, i.e. leaving in a huff, i.e. in high dudgeon, and Nirit gave us a discreet thumbs up through the pane of glass and mouthed the words *Amity raus!*

11

We were sitting in the seminar listening to Amity at the podium. This week was her turn to present her project. It wasn't the absolute worst talk I'd heard so far, the woman was verbally adept, and with so much uninterrupted speaking time she was setting a seminar record for "i.e." iterations – but her subject! An unsung proto-feminist Belgian lawyer from the nineteenth century now being elevated to the upper echelons of academic inquiry through Amity's superimposition of all kinds of high-theory garbage on what amounted to a plain-wrap biography of an utterly colorless figure. By comparison the Bratislava department-store talk had been nothing short of spellbinding. Then the usual discussion ensued – another female encounter group – and everyone praised Amity's historiographic puff-piece as pathbreaking scholarship. But hey gang, instead of everyone just nosing around in their petty little baili-wicks of research, could we have a meaningful discussion for a change? Address the larger issues for once? Inject some sweep and magnitude? Perchance a dollop of *humor*? I actually had no problem with feminism on the whole, I liked women being men's social equal, at very least it made things more intriguing, but the Amity Susskinds were making things more dull and ponderous . . . I'd had enough . . . my hand shot up . . . a wary look crossed Amity's face but still she nodded my way.

"Why does any of this matter?"

"Why does any of this *matter*?"

"Precisely."

"If you need to be told then I simply can't help you."

"You can help me by explaining."

"Next question."

The date for my paper had been set for just before New Year's Eve, it would be our last presentation before the long semester break, and that day the Frankelhirsch Library was packed. It wasn't just the usual seminar participants but the general public as well, a journalist from Israel's "paper of record" was even in attendance, and all this external interest was due to my topic: German elites jousting over women – metaphoric knights and literal *femmes fatales*. Something a discerning Jewish public could finally sink its teeth into. Miriam introduced me, I went into my talk and they were rapt, I have to say, I threw in some risqué humor that had them cackling, and their applause at the finish was loud and sincere. In her capacity as moderator Miriam did a nice synopsis, she posed some follow-up questions, then proceeded to field them from the audience. A few hands went up from the public, but seminar participants had precedence, so Miriam called on my biggest fan.

"I'd like to congratulate Dr. McIlhenny on quite the diverting talk," Amity said in a voice dripping with sarcasm. "I'm sure we were all very entertained, and your passion and enthusiasm for the subject is manifest. But I'm just wondering how a relative handful of German duelists and their hyperbolic masculine ethos can speak to us today – i.e. an anachronistic subcult, a historical curiosity, something now dead and gone and good riddance. In short, to employ your own famous words, why does any of this *matter?*"

The library held its breath – partly because they must have wondered why those words should have been famous . . .

"Well, Amity, if you don't care about love and death then what do you care about?"

Miriam squealed like a little girl, clapping her hands in delight, and the crowd erupted in relieved laughter. Amity didn't smile or frown or do anything really. What could she do, what can anyone do when a guy won't hoist on his own petard?

She left us the next day. It wasn't my doing unfortunately. From the start she had only planned on being with us for the fall semester because waiting for her in New England was a juicy tenure-track job at a very highbred school. At this point she had neither published her dissertation nor anything at all beyond a single "cutting-edge" article in a historical journal as obscure as her own Belgian feminist – so for someone who hated the old-boy network, our Amity had used the Ivy League version of it to admirable effect, and Bill Clinton's election later that year meant she didn't have to forsake America and her handsome little post.

12

All that fall I had planned on flying to Chicago for the NAH conference in late December, but the small problem was that no schools wanted to interview me. In fact the reason I delivered my talk in late December and not February, as originally planned, was that the woman scheduled for the December talk *had* gotten interviews, which she herself hadn't really foreseen since she was still ABD and neither a U.S. national nor native-English speaker and her applications more trial balloons than anything. But I had a mini-backup plan. I had applied for the post of a modern Europeanist at Amerophile College in Cairo and hadn't heard back from them one way or another. Their ad made no mention of interviewing applicants in Chicago, maybe they flew candidates into Cairo, and if so then I thought to save them the expense by hopping a bus and staging an ambush. At the same time I wanted to see King Tut, the Nile and Khufu/Cheops. As a world-history professor it behooved me to visit the cradle of civilization (or was that Mesopotamia?) so for 498 dollars I booked a week-long "budget tour" with an Egyptian travel company through its Israeli affiliate.

The bus left Yalom Eldad in the morning and we crossed the Sinai Peninsula, then the Suez Canal by barge, and under cover of darkness finally made Cairo. My hotel was the Al-Dajii and behind the reception desk was a wooden plaque with three stars nailed to it like some do-it-yourself job. Up in my room the bathroom had no hot water, no toilet paper, but what it did have was a massive cockroach roosting placidly on the inside wall of the tub. I wasn't going after the cockroach – the thing might attack *me* – but there was a mangy towel that looked like it had been a camel-saddle blanket in a previous life (or just used by previous guests as the toilet paper) so I shut the bathroom door and crammed the towel in the crack below the door. Before turning in for the night I whipped back the bedspread in anticipation of a roiling colony of vermin – nothing – and made minute inspection of the blanket and sheets, still nothing, then tore the bed apart and looked under the mattress.

All clear.

I climbed in and tried to sleep.

And did.

Maybe half an hour.

Music was coming from above me. Beating drums and crashing cymbals and the sound of flutes. I'd been told I had the top floor – was somebody on the roof? I had no urge to investigate, not barefoot with the light switch at the other end of this roach refugium, but it had been a long day and I shortly nodded off.

Next morning down at the reception desk they told me I was on the hotel's top floor, no mistake there, but two floors above me was a nightclub. I took another look at that "3-star" plaque. Most definitely counterfeit. Or in Egyptian hotels the stars were the number of inches on their bugs. While waiting in the lobby for my guide I found Amerophile College on a map, it was downtown, but we wouldn't be anywhere near downtown today. My guide came in smoking a cigarette, a slim mustachioed guy who spoke good English, then we got in his little Peugeot and I asked where we were headed.

"Many places," he said. "It will be a surprise."

"Have you been doing this kind of work long?"

"This is not my work, I'm a doctor."

"What kind of doctor?"

"A gynecologist."

"No market these days for gynecologists?"

"There are too many of us."

"Since the Egyptian women are so beautiful."

"We don't look at their faces."

He prepped me with Egyptological mumbo-jumbo – Old, New and Middle Kingdoms – dynasties and nomes – pharaohs, gods and burial rites. We crossed the Nile and saw a massive red-granite likeness of Ramses II, we traveled into the desert to Zoser's famous stepped pyramid, then drove to the Sphinx and the three big pyramids.

"You want to visit a burial chamber?"

"Will I see mummies?"

"Who knows."

He took me to one of the smaller pyramids with an entrance at its base and motioned me to go first. I stooped and entered the passageway. It wasn't more than five-feet high and angled into the earth below the base of the pyramid. I crept downward while other people came back up, a tiny dark space clogged with sweaty human bodies that made the air thick and fetid. I felt the onset of panic. But I had to say I'd seen the pharaoh's burial chamber – and couldn't turn back now with the guide right behind me. Finally the chamber came and I popped out the opening and straightened up and looked around.

Empty.

Just a cleaned-out vault. I stood waiting for my guide, but he didn't emerge from the tunnel, then more tourists came but still no guide. I clambered back up the passageway. When I reached the top gasping for air I saw my guide standing there coolly smoking his cigarette.

"Did you see it?"

"There was nothing there."

"Grave robbers plundered it a thousand years ago."

The guy wasn't a gynecologist but a comedian.

That second night in the Al-Dajii the music was even louder than before. I had been planning to drop by Amerophile College the next day before catching my train to Luxor, but finally closing my eyes at 3 a.m. put the kibosh on that one. I slept for most of the train ride which lasted six hours. Walking down the platform of the Luxor station, I was approached by a young guy in a Planet Hollywood T-shirt.

"You are Dr. McIlhenny?"

"Yes, and I'm no gynecologist."

"I am from the Hotel Hatshepsut, may I take your bag?"

Out front of the station the kid had a tiny motorcycle and he put my bag on his lap while I got on behind. We zipped through Luxor traffic, missing cars by half-inches, but finally made the hotel in one piece. At the reception desk they recommended a good restaurant for dinner, I had stuffed pigeon, then back at reception I left a wake-up call for 6:30 a.m. and next morning was jerked awake by a violent pounding on my door.

"Who's there?"

"6:30 o'clock – wake up!"

"Thanks!"

I lifted the receiver of the telephone next to the bed. It had a dial tone. I replaced the receiver, pondered it awhile, then gave up.

The kid rode me out on his motorcycle to the Nile, where I got ferried across, and waiting on the opposite bank was my guide. He was son of a native Egyptologist who had dug with "Mr. Carter," the Englishman who exhumed Tutankhamen in 1922, and we got this from the guide personally – "we" because this leg of the tour I was accompanied by a couple from Tennessee. It was kind of touching because the wife was blind, the husband played seeing-eye dog, and I wondered if he described our guide to her since the man was a sight. He wore an outfit which looked off-the-rack Banana Republic, complete with pith helmet, and he wielded a horsehair flyswatter that he swished to and fro above his head whenever he temporarily lost us among the legions of tourists tramping like miniature armies across this necropolis of 65 pharaoh tombs. He lectured on cartouches, hieroglyphs, Osiris the underworld god, Horus the falcon god (by this point I knew exactly how my students must have felt) and the hands-down most impressive thing was how he always worked "my father's old colleague Mr. Carter" into the monologue.

That evening I caught the night train for Aswan and next morning was met at the hotel by my Nubian guide, Abdullah, who was affable and relaxed and just took me around and showed me stuff without giving a lecture each time. We saw the Aswan Dam and rode a motorboat to an island with a Greek temple, we headed to another island where Lord Kitchener had lived, then finished off the day by visiting Aga Khan's mausoleum. Abdullah explained that the Aga Khan had founded a religion which people still believed in and that he was father of Ali Khan, the international playboy who married Rita Hayworth, who was someone I had always believed in.

That evening the travel company's Aswan agent escorted me to the train station for the trip back to Cairo. He wore a white suit and was nervous-looking and maybe even expecting trouble because when we got to the station there was no ticket waiting for me. The agent threw his weight around, got a note from the stationmaster, then we boarded the train and on the strength of this improvised voucher he tried to kick one of the passengers out of his seat. The passenger was a turbaned fellow, stuck in his belt was one of those giant knives in its curling silver sheath, and the guy wasn't budging. Voices were raised and the turbaned party shot me murderous looks. My agent turned on his heel and we exited the car and he rushed back to the stationmaster's office while I waited on the platform. Passengers stared out their windows. Eventually my agent emerged from the stationmaster's office with FIVE hard-faced officials who marched into the car while I remained on the platform. I could see them gesticulating. Other passengers were jumping out of their seats and waving their hands, the whole car rising up in defense of their compatriot against the foreign infidel, and my phalanx of officialdom finally retreated. As the agent went past I grabbed his arm.

"Hey, I can take the next train."

I didn't savor the notion of some guy who looked like the sultan's henchman being ousted from his seat just so my agent could preserve his reputation with the Cairo home office. The train had already been held up ten minutes – they delayed its departure on my account – and also unappealing was the prospect of traveling the length of Egypt with a compartment full of rancorous Muslim faithful.

"No!" said my agent. "That is your seat!"

"But it's his dagger."

"Please?"

"There's another train in two hours, book me on that."

"You are a gracious man."

Scared-shitless man. I slept for most of the sixteen-hour ride back to Cairo, though not at daybreak since that's when a guy burst into our car and sounded a shrill call to prayer. I was ready to hit the aisle on all fours and pay homage to Mecca, but no one unfurled their prayer mat or even moved except to shift with annoyance in their seat, then the character left and snoring recommenced.

After arrival in Cairo I spent the rest of the day recovering from the train ride, then waking up in the Al-Dajii my final morning I looked out the window and saw the city shrouded in a yellow haze. Down at the reception desk I was told that Cairo had been hit by a sandstorm, which happened every year or so and typically ushered in the spring, but this occurrence was especially bad and early. I walked onto the street and could make out large objects 200 yards away, but anything a quarter-mile distant just vanished. That meant the sun too. Not a good day for contact-lens wearers, of which I was one, so the white headcloth I had bought in Luxor now came in handy as I wrapped my face with a slit for the eyes then mounted my shades and was Claude Rains. I had planned to visit the Egyptian Museum but now struck that from my agenda and lit out straight for Amerophile College.

Getting around in a sandstorm is tough. I tried taking underground passageways but they were choked with dust. I finally made it to the university's main building which looked like a Moorish palace. I went through the door and unwound my headcloth but unbelievably the sand had made its way into the building. Everything had a fine film over it. I walked along the inlaid marble floor down a corridor and at the end was a door which said DEAN'S OFFICE. As good a place to start as any. I knocked, a voice said come in, and I entered an outer office with a carved wooden desk and a striking Egyptian-looking woman behind it and one guy standing and another guy sitting with his thigh propped on the desk corner.

"Hope I'm not disturbing anything."

"How can we help you?" said the sitting guy.

I stated my name and mission.

"You hit the jackpot," he said now gesturing toward the standing fellow. "This is Professor Sherman from the history department. He's heading the search committee."

Sherman came over and shook my hand. "And this is Dean Unseld," he said gesturing to the sitting guy who now gained both feet and shook my hand.

"And I'm his secretary," said the woman rising from her seat and reaching her hand across the desk.

This was all very chummy. Through dumb luck I'd cut through the paperwork and bureaucracy and corralled the main actors. My audacity was paying off.

"So I presume the job hasn't been filled yet," I said.

"No," said Sherman.

"And you weren't in Chicago interviewing candidates?"

"Oh yes, but frankly we weren't bowled over."

I was getting them on the rebound, which was perfect, as no department wanted to restart a search if something just dropped in their lap.

"And apparently not bowled over by my application," I said, "since I didn't even get to the interview stage."

"Not at all," said Sherman. "I remember your application quite well – among the better ones in fact."

"So I'm giving you a second chance."

They laughed.

"You're too kind," said Sherman. "But we're looking for an early-modern Europeanist and not a late-modern one."

It would have been nice if they had mentioned that in their ad, which only specified "Modern Europe," but no sense taking issue now, so I said goodbye and returned to the sandstorm.

13

The seminar started up again – then mercifully ended three months later. All told it had been a pretty lackluster affair. Everyone was so busy subverting paradigms and reframing narratives that I could barely recall what their subject matter was. But one of the papers had been hard to forget, given by a guest speaker who had the good taste and judgment to pick away at a pimple high on his domed forehead as he spoke, and it eventually burst and blood trickled down and was about to plunge over the cornice of his shaggy eyebrow into his jaundiced academic eye, when Miriam stepped forward and offered the casualty a kleenex to daub his wound.

"Let me help illustrate your thesis," she said.

He had been speaking of South African women as "caregivers" in their function as nurses in the Boer War. He was embarrassed but succeeded in stanching the sticky flow for a time, but then the pimple *reburst* with the blood surging forth. If and when to step in again? Upon reaching his eyebrow? Or would it dam up there this time and we could just let things be and have him sit there for the rest of his talk with a red pinstripe down his forehead? I was fervently praying for this latter version, but before it made his eyebrow our caregiver Miriam intervened anew.

The gory zit had been the highlight of our six-month seminar.

Too bad Jeremy wasn't on hand to experience it. He had left for America some time before due to family obligations, so Miriam dug up an extra 1200 dollars so I could make up his share of the rent for another couple months while plotting my next move. I had the vague notion of getting some stopgap position in Israel because once you left the academic loop, if only for a year, it was tough to break back in. There was so much competition on the market that a year of no formal affiliation rendered you "unserious" as a professional scholar. But even if I didn't land a slot somewhere, I was certain that Miriam would let me stay and use the letterhead from the INSTITUTE FOR WOMEN'S STUDIES AND FEMALE EMPOWERMENT on my job applications and keep the university as my mailing address. She had already been generous with the 1200 bucks as well as giving me the key to the Frankelhirsch so I could work there after hours, which is how I fell into conversation with a certain Judith – pronounced "Yoodit" – who wasn't quite done perusing her microfilm one Friday afternoon as they were closing up, so I told Nirit she was with me.

"And you trust this guy?" she said to Judith. "He could be a psychopathic rapist."

"I don't think he's a rapist," she said.

"But who's to say not a psychopath."

"Hey Nirit, what did I ever do to you?"

A couple hours later Judith and I were taking the bus. In Israel the buses shut down for Shabbat from sunset Friday to sunset Saturday, but it was spring now and dusk had been pushed back, so the buses were running later and we snagged one. It also happened that Judith lived just one street over from me. She was presently heading to an appointment with "Doron," her psychoanalyst, but she proposed I come by for a visit afterward.

At nine o'clock I walked over to her street but couldn't locate the address she'd given me. I returned to my flat. I couldn't call her since we hadn't exchanged phone numbers, so I cracked a Goldberg and thought about it. In the Frankelhirsch we had fallen into conversation because I was working on that part of my dissertation which dealt with Arthur Schnitzler's literary treatment of dueling and honor, Judith said she adored Schnitzler, particularly his *Reigen*, a play about sex and eroticism in fin-de-siècle Vienna, she herself a *Wienerin*, we'd spoken German and she had that saucy Viennese lilt, then of course her psychoanalysis, it was almost too perfect, from the city of Freud who'd called Schnitzler his doppelgänger . . .

Someone was ringing downstairs. I got on the intercom and it was Judith. I buzzed her up.

"It was a Freudian slip," she said when I opened the door.

"What was?"

"Giving you the wrong address."

"You *knew* it was the wrong address?"

"Only afterward with Doron. But I realized why – I want to move beyond codes. I didn't want you getting the wrong idea."

"Not sure I get the idea now."

"The codes. I want to transcend them. And I have a feeling you don't or can't."

"Come in and we'll transcend the codes sitting down."

"I have to go," she said. "I just wanted to tell you that."

Two days later the buses were running again – the work week in Israel is Sunday to Thursday – and when I got to the Frankelhirsch she was in the microfilm cubicle again.

"Hello."

"Hello."

I took a seat at my computer several cubicles down.

"Maybe lunch?"

I looked over. "Maybe lunch what."

"Would you like to have lunch with me."

"Not another Freudian slip?"

"No," she laughed. "And not a code either. I'm sorry about Friday night, I can explain everything."

She didn't like the food at the university cafeteria, a couple nearby restaurants had Russian waitresses whom she also didn't care for, so we headed to a seaside place in her hatchback.

"You know," she said over our meal, "I felt a little funny when that librarian called you a rapist. I work a rape-crisis hotline. I know how these things start and didn't want you to think that coming up to my apartment meant you were coming into my bed."

"A code for sex."

"That's right."

"Well, in my circles it's not a code, it's more or less a written invitation."

"I was right to be careful."

"Of course."

"Though *you* don't believe that."

"Not me, but most guys."

"That's exactly what the literature says – most men are potential rapists."

"And all people are potential killers."

"What's that got to do with it?"

"That all people are capable of all manner of things. The point is that despite the potential, most men *aren't* rapists."

"So we should award you a medal? Men see women as sex objects."

"Because their object is sex – it's nature at work."

"It's *nurture* at work. The male gaze is socially learned . . ."

I finally got her talking about herself. She was Jewish as surmised, both her parents Jews, but had she been brought up in the Jewish faith? No, they were secular Jews, which didn't imply she wasn't *culturally* Jewish.

"What's that mean?"

"It's hard to explain."

"Let me help," I said. "You're alienated from the hegemonic gentile world, you feel like the disempowered Other, and this combined with your gender makes you feel not only marginalized but stripped of proactive agency and why you need psychoanalysis. Am I getting warm? Shall I continue?"

She said continue. As I spoke she remained quiet, perhaps my jokey guesswork flat wrong, but there was a shine of admiration in her eyes. I had learned my parlance well – who knew that the Frankelhirsch seminar would aid in my seduction technique?

We went for a stroll on the beach. She told me how she had journeyed to Israel two years ago after falling in love with a young Israeli soldier. They had been part of an international Jewish youth group that was visiting historical Jewish sites in Eastern Europe, she followed him back to Yalom Eldad, and a few months later he dumped her.

"That's the main reason I began seeing a psychoanalyst."

"Are you making any progress?"

"It's not a question of progress."

"What then?"

"Just keeping my sanity."

A couple nights later she called and asked if I wanted to come over and look at some rape literature.

"Then I'll need your real address."

Her place was nice. It had plush furniture, glass-topped tables, Persian throw rugs on the off-white carpet and framed oil paintings on the walls. The only work Judith did was for the rape-crisis hotline, which was on a volunteer basis, and judging solely from the apartment and its furnishings then those monthly checks she got from her doctor mother and jurist father had to be pretty generous. Her rape literature was more feminist stuff – it turned out she was writing her bachelor's thesis on some aspect or other of the Israeli women's movement – and for half an hour I toughed it out but then patience ran low and I asked if a guy couldn't have a drink. She reached for a cut-glass decanter of brandy that tasted like apricot-flavored cough syrup, and we worked on that for a while, listening to a couple Beethoven quartets, and then fell into an embrace.

No kissing though.

"I have to be free to kiss someone."

"Who says you're not."

"But I wouldn't mind if you spent the night."

"Not some coded message?"

"Spending the night means spending the night."

"On the couch?"

"In bed. With me. But don't expect too much."

This seemed like a matchless prescription for blue-balls and I said no.

Next night she invited me over for a "study break." We talked and cuddled and again she asked me to spend the night – while once more adding that I shouldn't expect too much – but this time I went along with the stunt since I thought a second refusal would be both rude and impolitic. She went to bed in a T-shirt and thong and let me fool around from the waist up, but that was it, and no kisses from her in return. We spent a fun, frustrating, giggly, ludicrous night entwined in each other's arms and legs with no mutual kissing let alone penetration. It was the worst of both worlds. Like being with a prostitute who didn't kiss her clients and a virgin who kept her legs clamped shut. The entire time she was on call for the rape-crisis hotline, the phone right near her bed, and it hadn't rung all night but then finally did.

"Let me take it," I said. "You know, give them the man's perspective for a change – "

"No!"

She was some time on the phone. What I wanted to

tell the woman at the other end was that she shouldn't even kiss a guy since it might become passionate and lead to sex, which was how I rationalized Judith's thinking and continued to do so as the days wore on and the nights wore me out, these kissless and fuck-less events where each time the phone rang the thought invaded my mind that somewhere in Israel was a real man not standing for such antics and showing some cojones.

14

Aside from Miriam and Jeremy, Shoshana was about the only seminar participant I had any real respect for. She was an Israeli who spoke beautiful British-accented English and always had something both trenchant and highly pertinent to say each week. Well-spoken, incisive, no-nonsense – an academic of the best kind – and she also had a killer chassis. I don't know why there was no sexual pull between us, maybe she was too brainy for me, but in any case it seemed we both wrote each other off as bedmates without discarding the notion of friendship and as it turned out flatmates since now I was moving in with her.

Shoshana charged me only nominal rent for her extra room, but what it needed was a mattress. Judith had an old ratty one lying around, so we piled it in her hatchback and drove the few blocks to Shoshana's place. Once we got the thing in, Judith didn't stay long. I could tell that she and Shoshana weren't hitting it off.

"So that was Judith," I said when she finally made tracks. "What do you think?"

"Pretty," said Shoshana.

"That it?"

"Well, if you want to know the truth, I can't imagine someone more unsuitable for you."

Trenchant.

Not that the unsuitable Judith would have wanted to spend Passover with me anyhow, but it was Shoshana who invited me to her family's celebration. They lived an hour south of Yalom Eldad by bus, I was greeted at the terminal by Shoshana who had arrived home the day before, and we drove the short distance to her house where I met the family and their guests and things kicked off. I wore a white yarmulke embroidered with silver and sat politely while Moses freed the Israelites and we the captive audience gnawed flat stale bread and drank wine that tasted like Welch's grape juice. An elderly gentleman with an Oxbridge accent kept me in suppressed laughter the whole time as he mocked the ceremony and whispered bawdy jokes in my ear. Next morning we all sat around and sipped coffee while some people left and new people arrived. One of the fresh arrivals was a guy named Avi who worked as master of ceremonies at a Yalom Eldad cabaret, but it was less this fact than simply his speech and demeanor which gave rise to certain inferences, though his black pompadour wig also had my gaydar on high alert. Avi was interested to hear I was an Angeleno since he hailed from L.A. too.

"You've heard the joke," he said. "Why Yalom Eldad and L.A. are so alike? Palm trees, beaches, beautiful weather, gorgeous suntanned people . . . just more Jews in L.A."

"Rimshot."

"Don't mind if I do."

After a while he stood up to go and asked if I needed a ride back north.

"I'm getting one from Shoshana, thanks."

"Oh Steve!" called Shoshana from across the room.

"That would actually be brilliant. I'd like to stay another day or two if you don't mind – I'm not quite ready to face Yalom Eldad again."

Since when was Yalom Eldad so rough? Palm trees, beaches . . .

"No problem," I said. "I'll catch the bus."

"You silly," said Avi. "The buses don't run on Shabbat."

I had meant that evening. But Shoshana didn't jump in with an offer to stay till then, so I accepted Avi's offer. His transport was a red motorscooter and he had an extra helmet for just such occasions, but what he didn't have was a sissy bar in back for me to grip, so I had to wrap my arms around his soft belly.

"Hang on tight!"

The entire trip he wriggled his butt into my lap to evoke a surge of interest. I mean he really *ground* it in there. I'll jump from this scooter and risk life and limb, I thought desperately, before I get aroused. His helmet swiveled around:

"Would you like to make a quick stop in Yirtak?"

Yirtak was a quaint Arab enclave just south of Yalom Eldad. After one of our seminars Miriam had taken the whole group there for dinner. I told Avi I'd already been.

"Not to my houseboat you haven't!"

He didn't leave me much choice. The boat was tied up at one of the harbor's long wooden docks. No sooner were we below deck when Avi offered to perform fellatio on me.

"Thanks, I'm a confirmed heterosexual."

"Oh, is that all," he said. "I specialize in you confirmed types. What's the matter, you got a girlfriend?"

For the sake of argument I said yes.

"You don't know what you're missing."

"You're right I don't."

"So what are we waiting for?"

"A change in my sexual orientation, I believe."

"You want a beer? Let me get you a beer."

The guy had done me a favor and I needed his good offices for the rest of the trip into town. He went into the kitchen and came out with glasses and a couple beers.

"I don't need a glass."

"How butch."

I took a long swig.

"So tell me about your girlfriend."

I gave him the specs on Judith.

"Does Judith go down on you?"

"And if I said yes?"

"Judith can't give head like I can. Women don't like giving blowjobs. They don't know what makes a good one."

I killed my beer, figuring this was the hour glass of our little encounter.

"You drank that fast," said Avi. "You need another one."

"What I need is to get back to town."

"You have time for one more."

He swished back to the galley and returned with another beer and some color prints.

"Look at this," he said handing me a snapshot of himself in nothing but his Elvis wig. "Kenny took that. He's blond and athletic like you. You want to see Kenny?"

He handed me a picture of Kenny who was big – 6'8" – and had his clothes on. Or rather his uniform. I knew this Kenny. I'd seen him on TV playing basketball for Yalom Eldad's pro team.

"Kenny's married," said Avi. "But he doesn't get the loving he needs from his wife. He comes to me for that."

"A real bitch, huh."

"Flattery will get you everywhere."

"I mean the wife."

"Aren't they all? But your girlfriend, Judith, she's not a bitch I suppose."

"The jury's still out."

"It doesn't sound like you're in love."

"I run hot and cold with her."

"How are you running now?"

"Lukewarm."

"You're a real tease, you know that?"

It was another hour before we finally got out of there, my heterosexuality intact, and he rode me the rest of the way to Yalom Eldad without any more butt grindings, which was vaguely disappointing.

15

Then Judith warmed up to me – likely because I had moved in with Shoshana and observed Passover with her family. It was curious how these feminists, who believed a woman needed a man like a fish needed a bicycle, got jealous when another fish swam into the picture, no matter how platonic the relationship.

That was my interpretation because we finally had sex. Sort of.

We had gone to a non-Russian-waitress restaurant and Judith looked nice in a black bolero jacket and swishy black-satin pantalons. When we got home she opened a bottle and we listened to a CD she had of great operatic tenors and I explained the difference between the lyric and spinto styles. Then we took turns reading from a comic play by the nineteenth-century Austrian dramatist Johann Nestroy. Occasionally we stopped and Judith clarified some of the more idiomatic German wordplay. I didn't find Nestroy that funny but still chortled along with Judith, who found him riotous and my own diction wanting.

"Let me read from now on," she said. "When you speak German you sound like a Nazi."

We had spoken almost exclusively German to this point in our association. Was she hearing Julius Streicher every time I opened my mouth? And kept it to herself?

Admirable forbearance!

"I only noticed it now," she said. "This is Viennese dialect and you're not even close."

"Granted."

"Just let me read."

Afterward we hit the sack. All these weeks I had wondered what would happen first – coition or osculation – though by this time we had graduated to a bit of teasing lip and tongue play, albeit nothing deep or sustained, when suddenly she whispered:

"There are condoms in the nightstand."

Maybe Nazi accents turned her on. I found a packet and tore it open and fumbled with the condom . . . crunch time . . . zero hour . . . and it wouldn't go on. In just fifteen seconds I had gone from *Weltmacht* to *Niedergang*. I revived things to the point where I was able to wrestle the condom into place, though it was all pretty mushy down there, and Judith monitored the operation with an unblinking gaze while offering no comment. Where was the rape-crisis hotline when you needed it? Ring telephone ring! Then I focused all my being into that malingering appendage and it was triumph of the will which finally got the deadbeat inserted. But try to keep a failing erection with a rubber on, a fairly thick one as far as I could judge, so a minute later I exited and stripped it off.

"I can't feel jack with these stupid condoms."

"Whatever you say."

I went to the bathroom and threw the killjoy in the trash. When I came back Judith had her eyes shut and was in the fetal position with her back to my side of the bed. Nothing coded in that.

16

When I woke the next morning she was bustling around the apartment. Today we were heading to the Judean Desert for three days, one of those Society for the Protection of Nature tours. It was something we'd planned two weeks before – to make an outing somewhere she hadn't been with her soldier boyfriend – and a couple weeks back it had seemed like a good idea. Now I rose from bed and walked into the shower and had just pulled the curtain when she yanked it aside and joined me under the water.

"We're running late."

We rubbed up against each other as we rubbed our own selves with liquid soap. She was all business, brisk and efficient, but it was still titillating, largely for that reason.

"Can you get my back?"

I lathered her back. Then I moved my lathering action downward and into her breach and inveigled a finger. She was as slick inside as out. My morning stiffy was poking her from behind as I reached around to fondle her breasts. There would be no repeat of last night. She turned to face me.

"I can do your back."

I turned around. That's right, heighten the foreplay, we're not running *that* late. She rubbed soap on my back then moved quickly past me and out of the shower.

Good girl, get that condom!

I washed off the soap and luxuriated in the hot stream and waited for her to reappear . . .

"Please finish showering! We'll miss the bus!"

17

The Judean Desert was a chalky white vastness. We did rappels down canyon walls, followed dried wadis, clambered up and down escarpments, then at sunset we pitched our tents. Judith and I slept in the same pup tent and she didn't slink out in the middle of the night like Margot Macomber, but that's about all she didn't do. We were in a group of some twenty people, all younger, and she flitted about and flirted with several of the men, one in particular with whom she exchanged phone numbers right in front of me.

That did it.

"And she lives at 28 Shalai Niron. Just in case you call and she gives you the wrong address. It's been known to happen."

The guy looked at me wonderingly. I had addressed him in English, he and Judith had been talking Hebrew, and now Judith snapped at me in German: "Was für ein blöder Spruch! Du kannst mal die Klappe halten und dich besser raushalten!"

Shut up and butt out and keep the stupid remarks to yourself!

"You know, Judith," I said back in her native tongue. "When you speak German you sound just like Magda Goebbels."

She didn't care for that either and made sure to air her annoyance. But leastwise the guy backed off. He smelled trouble and already had her number anyway.

Somehow we got through the next day and a half without any more blowouts, but on the bus ride home we had nothing to say to each other, and in the days following we again stayed out of touch. Though we might have anyway since it was a dual holiday. Israel had its Memorial Day and Independence Day back to back, which made sense, first honor your fallen soldiers then celebrate what they died for. Memorial Day was subdued but Independence Day the nation cut loose and the fireworks display that night was spectacular, exploding charges everywhere you looked, in a 360-degree panorama, and I went to the Kings of Israel Square for an unimpeded view and was attacked by kids squirting Silly String and bopping me on the head with squeaky plastic hammers. Now I was sitting in a café with Shoshana, who'd been away for the holidays, and I told her of being repeatedly assailed and even singled out.

"You reek of gentile."

"Not gentility?"

"Just be glad they didn't give the gentile one in the genitals."

"I'm watching out for you, Shoshana."

"As well you should, luv, as well you should."

I told her about Judith and the Judean Desert.

"She behaved rather badly," said Shoshana. "And I can't understand why – unless you're leaving something out."

I had left something out. The non-sex night before and the shower episode the next morning, which were just too embarrassing.

"There's no excuse for that kind of behavior," I said embarking on another rant, this one longer and above all louder, and Shoshana suggested I might keep it down.

"I don't care who hears."

"Even her?" said Shoshana. "She's sitting a couple tables behind you."

"You're joking."

"I'm not."

"Has she been there the whole time?"

"Yes."

"And you didn't tell me?"

"She's wearing sunglasses. I only recognized the woman after you started castigating her. But maybe she didn't hear you – she's been talking to her girlfriend the whole time."

Shoshana was getting me into some interesting jams. Avi the blowjob specialist and now this. I flagged down the waitress and ordered another beer.

"She's Russian," I said when she left with my order. "Judith hates Russian waitresses."

"That's one point in her favor."

"Meaning she shouldn't even be here."

"She won't be for long – they just asked Ludmilla for the check."

"Damn."

"Now or never."

"Are they coming our way?"

"No."

I didn't turn my head, just waited till they entered my field of vision. She was looking good, as they always do in these instances, her creamy complexion set off nicely by big round sunglasses like those styled by jetsetters on the Côte d'Azur, and she also wore the black bolero-pantalon combo – like a mocking reminder of my collapse that evening. She and her girlfriend chatted a bit more on the sidewalk, then they hugged and went their separate ways, Judith in direction of her apartment.

I took all this in since she never once looked my way.

"Is she gone?" said Shoshana. "Can we breathe easy again? You know it just occurred to me – you were talking about her the whole time so why shouldn't she have been talking to her girlfriend about you?"

"What are you saying?"

"That the very reason she didn't come over is she'd been going on about you all the while. Total conjecture on my part, but more than possible."

"You're pure evil, you know that?"

"It's been said before."

"So what do you suggest?"

"You could go after her."

"I don't go running after girls."

"She won't be running after you, luv."

"What makes you so sure."

"She didn't just now when she had the chance."

I drank off my Goldberg, left some money for Shoshana who wished to bask in the sun and her depravity, then raced after Judith. Her place was just a couple blocks away. I rang her apartment and she came on the intercom in Hebrew.

"Judith, it's me Steve, we need to talk."

She buzzed me in. I walked up the short flight of stairs and her door was ajar. When I entered, she was moving around the flat. "I'm late for Doron," she said. "We'll talk when I get back."

And she was gone.

The place had been given a good cleaning, things rearranged, a fresh smell in the air. I opened her bottle of Hungarian vodka and took a slug and lay down on the couch. I nodded off for a good long while, likely the result of emotional fatigue, then heard the rattle of keys in the door.

"How was Doron?"

"Fine," she said. "You had something you wanted to say?"

"Don't think I'm not aware of what you've done. I see the apartment – it's all cleaned up – as you've likely cleaned me out of your system and out of your life. At the café you completely ignored me. I had my back to you and it wasn't *my* job to make the first approach. You just let me sit there. A guy can put two and two together."

"Get to the point."

"We're through right?"

"It never occurred to me."

She said the reason she'd been so distant with me and flirtatious on the trip was the shower incident. Feeling her up and prodding her with that erection of which I was so "proud" after my "failure" the night before was "revolting."

"I wasn't proud, just excited," I said. "Any crime in that?"

"You want to have sex and we're missing our trip!"

She was galled at me finding her erotic and having

the male's involuntary physical response. We discussed it for the next two hours, I ended up spending the night, and she grew affectionate but no intercourse. She had an appointment early the following day and let me sleep in, which felt like a token of her renewed trust, and even though she didn't leave a key, her apartment was on an elevated first floor where you could hop from the balcony onto the ground, so I did that and walked a short ways to a flower shop and bought eighteen roses. Reentering by the balcony I stuck the roses in a vase, added a fond note, then closed the balcony door and left by the front one, which you simply pulled shut behind you for it to lock automatically, and the flowers did the trick since that night successful fornication took place.

18

I never thought a self-proclaimed feminist and invet-
erate man-mistruster like Judith would be susceptible
to something so corny as a plus-size bouquet of roses –
which in turn made me think that she might be like
other women and all her sexual prevarication and
skittishness was merely due to what she saw as my im-
pending departure. Judith wasn't going to invest herself
in a guy who was ultimately busting town. It got my
mind back to why I had stayed in Israel in the first place
– not to shtup Judith but score a job – which might then
have the reciprocal effect of helping things between me
and Judith.

On the job front I had certain local contacts: a couple
professors and the former Israeli ambassador to Austria.
The ambassador had gotten in touch after Israel's paper
of record did an interview with me, he'd read his
share of Schnitzler, and now he and I met for lunch. It
turned out he couldn't help with a job but the guy was
graceful and engaging, and Judith was impressed, so
not a complete waste of time. The couple professors
were both at Yahweh University in Jerusalem. I made
appointments with them as well as a visiting German
scholar whom I knew from Berlin. Judith had offered
me use of her car for the Jerusalem sortie, so I took
her to dinner the night before and sprang for a bottle
of red wine. In Israel they made you pay for the water,
which is why I never ordered it, but I liked my red

wine with water on the side, a habit from my Gallo-jug days.

"Don't tell me there'll be a charge though," I said to the waiter. "Not with this pricey bottle."

"There will of course be a charge."

"Are we in the middle of a drought or something?"

"You don't really want to take me out," said Judith after the guy left with our menus.

"What makes you say that?"

"You won't pay for basic *water*?"

"I told him to bring it."

"You made a fuss."

"I reserve the right to make a fuss. In all my life I've never paid for tap water – at least till I came to the land of milk and honey where water seems a scarcity."

The night was sexless and next morning I discovered that I had left my razor at Shoshana's apartment.

"You can't go to Jerusalem unshaven," said Judith.

"I'll swing by my place."

Instead, running behind schedule, I headed straight to Jerusalem and an hour later was sitting on the terrace of Yahweh University's cafeteria with its magnificent view of the Old City . . . and by late afternoon I was driving back to Yalom Eldad and had accomplished nothing. All three of my contacts had been friendly and sympathetic but what did I expect – that they would waltz me into a job? All they could say was that the market was hard to crack these days and they had heard of an opening for a Germanist at this or that place, you might look into it, they'd keep an ear to the rail for other potential slots, the same old tune, but what they must have been thinking was: *Brother, am I glad to have this BULLSHIT safely BEHIND me.* Now back in Yalom Eldad I refilled the gas tank then stopped at my apartment where I shaved, showered, got back in my suit, loosened my tie, then drove the five minutes to Judith's place where I put my Long-Hard-Day-At-The-Office act on. Not that I'd ever had one of those days. But over the years I'd seen my corporate father give this performance so often that I had the bushed resignation down pat. "It's pretty hopeless," I said taking a sip from the vodka on the rocks which Judith had poured for me to round out the picture. "No one could give me any leads. We're back to square one."

"So what are your plans?"

"Not sure exactly."

She went and put on Bruckner's fourth symphony then vanished into the kitchen and came back with a bowl of chocolates and a cup of coffee.

"See lots of pretty girls?" she asked.

"No one pretty as you."

"I don't like it when you try to flatter me."

"Just expressing my view."

"You think I'm pretty?"

"Would I be sitting here now if you weren't?"

"Do you think you're good looking?"

"Only you can answer that."

"I want *you* to answer it."

"If a more than pretty girl likes me, then I can't be Yasser Arafat."

It took some time but the upshot was that love, for her, occupied a plane of male beauty (a plane that both

Yasser and I had failed to attain) while she felt herself not quite pretty enough to attract great-looking guys. Her ambition exceeded her grasp, hence her grievance, hence the desperate shimmer in her eyes, hence that lost-waif look, hence her frustration this whole time and my ensuing difficulties with her.

"I apologize for not being handsome enough."

"But I like being with you."

"That's nice to know."

"Don't be angry."

"Who's angry? I find this very amusing. Someday I'll write a novel and put you in it and they'll say what a wild imagination to invent such an eccentric and even implausible character."

"Don't be funny."

"But you might have a tough time of it in Israel."

"What do you mean?"

I told her that considering the general arrogance of the male population, a fact she herself had advised me of, and considering the competition she faced from countless lovelies flouncing around, she might have a hard time upgrading.

"You could be right," she said. "I might have to leave Israel."

So there it was. I had spent the whole day strategizing ways of staying in Israel, in part because of her, while she'd spent the day entertaining thoughts, in part because of me, that now issued in her leaving the country.

I decided to beat her to it.

19

The next couple weeks I hunkered down in the Frankel-hirsch to put the finishing touches on my book. Before pulling up stakes I wanted to send the completed manuscript off to Nobleton, which in turn would forward it to two academic referees to decide my fate. Returning home evenings I stayed more or less sloshed and for some reason kept listening to Artie Shaw's *Frost on the Moon* with Helen Forrest on vocal. It got on Shoshana's nerves and one day she left a note saying she had nothing against drinking, certainly nothing against Artie Shaw, but please avoid going overboard when she was in the very next room.

A fair request.

Especially since it was her booze I was swilling.

To chase the alcohol with some nutrition, I became the regular customer of an Indian fast-food place. The owner liked me and would come to my table to gripe about the Ethiopians – this Lost Tribe of Israel should stay lost! One endearing thing about the country was that no Israeli seemed to like any other Israeli. I had also noted antagonisms between Sephardic and Ashkenazi Jews, there was almost universal hostility toward the draft-dodging ultra-Orthodox, and nobody cared for the newly arrived Russians – they didn't know how to work, had grown up in a communist system, were all a bunch of freeloaders! As if Israel hadn't foreign foes enough.

It was the day before my depature when Judith called and she was all business.

"I need my mattress back."

"I don't have a car, Judith, you're welcome to pick it up."

"Ask your Shoshana, she has a car."

"And both of them out of town right now."

"Then call a taxi, find a friend – just please return it."

"I'll lug it downstairs and load it in your hatchback. I'll bring it into your apartment. You driving over here is one-tenth the hassle I'll have in rustling up a taxi and tying it on the roof or whatever."

"I'm not retrieving my own mattress."

"I'm in the middle of packing, Judith."

"Whose problem is that? I was nice enough to loan you the mattress, and I thought you'd bring it back on your own. I obviously overestimated you."

Her mattress was just something she'd had in storage – and now she wanted this discard back and wouldn't lift a finger to expedite its return. A sheer power play on her part. I'd seen enough of them to recognize the pattern. I gave her both barrels. All the vituperation and bitterness came spewing forth. She stayed cool and more or less took it.

"Do you feel like a big strong man now? I want my mattress."

"Okay," I said. "Goodbye."

Hanging up the phone, I did feel like a big strong man and went out for one last wingding with the Goldbergs. Only one thing rankled – that she might have interpreted my final words as consent to do her bidding. I should have just said over and out. On my way to Ben Gurion the next day I had the cabdriver stop at her place and I dropped a note in her mailbox saying I had schlepped the mattress downstairs and it was sitting in my front courtyard and she could drive by anytime and get it. It was only because of Shoshana that I'd done even that much, since I didn't want Judith giving her any trouble.

20

On the flight I read Shoshana's going-away present, a book by Timothy Mitchell called *Blood Sport: A Social History of Spanish Bullfighting*. It was a scholarly work but free of jargon, not a whiff of theory, and going to the heart of things like a good *estocada*. Bullfighting was of moment since I was heading to Madrid where my Zafiro pal Joe Vasquez was on an illustrious Prescott Scholarship. He had spent the year living and working in El Escorial, a small town outside Madrid that was adjacent Phillip II's massive granite palace, and now his research was done and his wife and kid had returned to America – but he still had a month on the Prescott, which is where I came in, to help him wind down and blow off steam, and that's where the bullfights came in.

Joe picked me up at the airport and we took a cab to his new place. He had relocated from El Escorial to a roomy Madrid apartment just above a bar, conveniently enough, though it seemed like half of all Madrid apartments roosted above some kind of watering hole. The flat was on loan to him from a Spanish couple who always left the city in summer, and I soon found out why, since I'd never experienced such scalding dry heat. In Madrid you hung a load of freshly washed laundry out on the balcony and ten minutes later it was stiff on the line. America with all its advanced technology and manufacturing prowess had yet to produce a dryer of equal efficiency. For food we took loaves of cheap stale bread and a crate of tomatoes and sliced it all up and Joe made a giant vat of "gazpacho." Then he removed all but two shelves from the refrigerator and stuck the vat in, the other shelf for our beer, and the whole month we subsisted on liquid tomatoes and Mahou cerveza. Breakfast included. Though more like lunch since it was the rare occasion when we rose before noon. We always chowed in the livingroom with its cool flagstone floor and French doors open to the balcony, the sound of traffic seeping in along with the occasional light breeze, but the pitiless sunlight at bay. The apartment didn't have a functioning telephone because the couple had it automatically switched off when they went away for the summer.

"How do we communicate with people?"

"There's a telegraph office nearby."

"Come off it."

"That's how I stay in touch stateside."

"And here in Madrid?"

"Then we're talking carrier pigeon."

Joe was less interested in the bullfights than I was, but he had nothing better to do and so I hauled him to Las Ventas two or three times a week, where we drank more Mahou beer and munched corn nuts and shouted *olé* when called for. Up until now my sole experience of the bullfight had been Mexico, and the major difference between the Mexican and Spanish bullfights was the bulls. The animals I had seen in Tijuana and Ensenada were fast and nimble – after charging through the cape or muleta they pivoted on a dime for another pass – and this gave the Mexican fights more dynamism and punch than those I saw in Spain. The Mexican bulls also charged the picadores with no hesitation or prompting, whereas the big black Spanish bulls took a couple pics and this seemed to destroy their spirit. But the worst part was how the moment of truth got botched. The bulls were so big that the matadors had trouble getting their sword in over the horns, or so it seemed, because almost no bull was ultimately killed by the matador with his sword but rather in a graceless follow-up attempt with a crude implement called a *verdugo* or even in a third stab by a member of his entourage who dug a knife back of the bull's head to finally sever its spinal cord. Not pleasant to witness let alone repeatedly (six bulls per bullfight) and I told myself that after this trip I was swearing off bullfights forever (not that I kept my vow) since there were just too many disheartening aspects to the thing. It was like a woman who gave you an ecstatic thrill now and then but you had finally reached the stage where the emotional pain you underwent for that thrill simply wasn't worth it – in fact you realized it had *never* been worth it, that you'd merely been captive to a febrile addiction – but as one will a past love, I found myself defending the bullfights at a Prescott event with Joe.

"And have you enjoyed what you've seen so far?" sneered one of America's best and brightest, having never himself attended a *corrida de toros.*

"Not on the whole," I said. "Most of the bulls aren't killed very cleanly. But when it's a good *faena,* and the sword hits home, it can be glorious."

"Glorious?" chimed in a woman Prescotter who was likewise completely innocent of bullfights. "*Glorious?*"

"Yes," I said. "Which is saying a lot about something that has so many noxious aspects."

"I'd say that calling bullfights glorious says a lot about *you*."

"What it says about Steve is that he's a serious scholar of archaic rites," said Joe. "He wrote his dissertation on the German duel. He's getting insight into the process of modern ritual violence."

"Try modern ritual butchery," said the woman.

"Butchery is a meat cow going straight to the slaughterhouse," I said now falling back on Tim Mitchell. "Give me the life of a fighting bull any day. They live twice as long, run free on pastureland, and can even survive the ring and be put out to stud for the rest of their natural lives."

"How do they survive the ring?" she demanded.

"If a bull is especially brave then the crowd can call for it to be spared."

"I'm sure that happens like almost never."

"But they have a fighting chance. And even if they don't survive, they get to die nobly in battle and not abjectly in the stockyard."

"You've read too much Hemingway."

"And you should first see a bullfight before you dump all over it."

"I don't need to see a summary execution to know it's a grotesque travesty."

"Maybe you're afraid you'll like it."

"I'd like it if I saw the matador die."

"You wouldn't say that if you saw it happen."

"Oh yes, I would."

In the bodega afterward it was just me and Joe, and I asked him why the half dozen Prescotters I'd met so far hadn't witnessed a single bullfight. This seemed improbable since they were all Iberianists and the very thing that had lured me to Spain didn't interest them in the slightest.

"A lot of Spaniards haven't either," he said. "Bullfighting was encouraged by Franco, he enshrined it as this deeply Spanish thing, so right-thinking libs can't like it."

"They see it as fascist."

"Correct as in politically so."

Another Prescott gathering took place in an apartment overlooking the Plaza Mayor, where the Spanish Inquisition had staged its torture and executions, and from high up you could see it was paved in a repeating pattern of crosses. The apartment belonged to a member of the American embassy who supervised the Prescott program in Madrid. He was a pleasant middle-aged guy, alert and receptive, so I tried him on bullfights.

"Sure, I like bullfights," he said. "How about you?"

"That's why I'm here."

"Mostly novilladas right now. You should come during the San Isidro festival in May and June. A bullfight every day, a month straight of tauromachy, best matadors in the world."

"But not the best bulls."

"You have the best breeders then too."

I told him about the Mexican bulls.

"But it's even tougher to work bulls that aren't perfectly brave," he replied. "They're an uncertain quantity since they don't charge as straight and predictably. It's the difference between hitting a fastball and a knuckler."

He knew a thing or two. Which gave me hope for the American diplomatic corps. I'd also liked the Israeli ambassador to Austria, that little genius Scheherazade had been some consul's kid, and I'd always had a glamorous image of diplomats – bon vivants and men-about-town – an image doubtless commandeered from Hollywood films like *The Merry Widow*, but if good enough for Lubitsch then it was good enough for me.

"How do you get in?"

"You start by taking an exam."

"And what's the starting salary?"

"$30,000. But it goes up quickly enough. You won't starve."

"Any choice where you're sent?"

"You bid on jobs. But also go where you're sent. Either that or resign."

"What was your first assignment?"

"Tehran."

"Were you in the hostage crisis?"

"Personnel transferred me out just before the revolution."

"Beirut here I come."

"If it's Lebanon then you might do only two years – four years max."

"Sounds like a prison sentence."

"I'm giving the diplomatic corps a bad name," he laughed. "The lifestyle has its downside, though on the whole it's very attractive."

"Like postings in Madrid."

"There are worse fates.

21

My last days in Madrid, I crossed things off the checklist I'd been neglecting for beer and bullfights. I finally saw Picasso's *Guernica* – young stoner vagabonds in tie-dye or Che Guevara T-shirts taking their seat on the floor in front of it and reclining against grubby backpacks and dreaming of the revolution – then I visited the Prado and saw Ribera and Goya, who were all the dream I needed. I rode out on the train with Joe to El Escorial, and after touring the palace we rendezvoused with a couple of his drinking pals, had a convivial Spanish evening, then he and I traveled back to Madrid in a semi-stupor and next day walked off our hangovers in the El Retiro park. We stopped at a shady café opposite the monument to Alfonso XII, which stood at edge of an artificial lake, and we ordered some hair of the dog.

"Why was this Alfonso guy such a big deal?" I asked.

"He died young."

"That all?"

"He was well liked."

Alfonso's equestrian statue was mounted on a high ornate pedestal backed by a crescent-shaped colonnade. It was quite the handsome monument. Dying young and well liked went a long way in Spain. People sat on the monument's steps leading down to the green lake, which had a smattering of rowboats, each of them with a female in the stern and some guy manning the oars.

A beggarwoman came by our table asking money for her *niños*, and Joe gave her 25 pesetas.

"Starting to, though not the States," he said when I asked if he missed his family. "It's funny but I *like* having no telephone. Or a car for that matter. I like walking to places, enjoy that afternoon siesta. Everything at a human pace. But now we have to go back to it – cars, Disneyland, shopping malls – the whole plastic, automated U.S. scene."

"Speak for yourself."

"You trying to find a job in Europe?"

"They've got plenty of Europeanists in Europe. Maybe if I was a specialist in Postcolonial Ibero-American Subaltern Studies it'd be a different story."

"Hey watch it."

"Just saying."

"Find your own hustle."

"I'm open for suggestions."

"Then keep with the whole women's history thing," he said. "Market yourself as someone who does women's history – only if you want a job of course."

"Then I'll have to keep that pose for the rest of my career."

"Just till you get tenure – then drop the pose and do whatever you damn well please."

"Tenure can be a long time coming."

"Less long for feminist historians. I know one woman who got tenure before forty."

"Who? Where?"

He told me.

"I'm sure her being Hispanic didn't hurt either," I said.

"I hope not."

"You can bank on it."

"I am," said Joe.

"And what about my dissertation on the manly art of dueling?"

"You can flip that around too. It's not some macho account of testosterone-driven jerks but GENDER STUDIES."

"I already pitched it that way to Nobleton."

"You're not as dumb as you look."

"And not so dumb as to think that some search committee would hire a dude for its women's history slot."

"You're right. But work the Gender Studies angle. It's a made-up field so make things up as you go along. You can already fake it with the double-talk and you just had six months of feminist theory."

"And feminist practice with Judith."

"I rest my case."

22

After a few days back home in Los Angeles I got the promised letter from my Madrid diplomat in which he gave me contact info for the diplomatic-corps exam. I hated exams, I was sick of taking exams, it seemed my whole life had been one endless examination to move from each stage of it to the next, but there was one scheduled for November so I signed up.

Meanwhile, as ever, there was the money problem.

For the first time in my life I visited the unemployment office. It was in Canoga Park, just a short drive, and an hour later I had made arrangements to receive a thousand dollars per month for the next year. I was amazed how easy it was – and how much they were willing to fork over. The thousand dollars was the most you could receive and was based on my last salaried position, which had been the dual teaching post at Zafiro/Bonita and the most I'd ever earned, and to keep the monthly grand coming all I had to do was send out three job applications per week. Universities were already advertising for professorships in the run-up to the 1992 NAH convention in December, there were at least a dozen openings for Europeanists in the NAH newsletter each month, so I was able to keep the unemployment office satisfied. The beauty of it all was that even if I got the offer of a job, then it would only begin in September 1993 – right when my unemployment checks ran out – so I could garner generous benefits for the entire 52 weeks permissible.

My dueling manuscript was still undergoing peer review, I could do nothing but wait, and I registered for a creative-writing course through UCLA extension. The class was Tuesday nights and taught by a Vietnam vet who had published some short stories about his wartime experience. That qualified you to teach creative writing at the university level? But he had a plainspoken and unassuming style that I liked. We read one of his own short stories along with Hemingway's *In Another Country* as examples in the art of simplicity and avoiding abstractions and creating a solid visual image with your writing – which was the exact opposite of the academic prose I'd been steeped in all these years. Instructive too was that you learned *nothing* from class critiques of your writing since no one knew what the hell they were talking about. I would have profited more from a correspondence course, just me and the teacher, and any fool could guess that this was an L.A. writing class since so much of the action took place in cars or started out that way: "Janet waited for the light to turn green and then depressed the accelerator as she rode smoothly over the intersection to her date with destiny . . ." Or: "He exited the Harbor Freeway and crossed Figueroa to South Olive then motored down to Fifth Street where he stopped in front of a one-hour parking meter . . ."

Write what you know – they'd taken that one to heart.

One Saturday that fall I depressed the accelerator and motored downtown for the diplomatic-corps exam. They gave us three hours to complete the thing. By the two-hour mark half the hall had emptied while I stayed till the end, so if they were grading on a curve then I was likely sunk since the failure rate was 80 percent, but a couple weeks later they told me by mail that I passed. Along with the good news they sent a sheaf of forms and stressed that because only 10 percent of those filling out the forms would proceed to the oral exam, your five-page biography is critical! I had written countless of these for academic-related stuff over the years but couldn't just recycle the old bios now because they focused on my education and scholarship. The diplomatic corps wanted life experience and intangibles of character. Or so I guessed. At first I gave it some hard thought – then just relaxed and was honest. I talked about selling my surfboard in the summer of 1988 to help supplement my doctoral grant for Berlin, which in hindsight seemed a regrettable shift in priorities; about choosing the topic of dueling for my dissertation not because of any socio-political concerns but since it was redolent of romance; about spending a month in Madrid going to bullfights on the pretext of studying deadly honorific rites, but in truth to indulge my taste for old-fashioned pageantry and valor . . . and the diplomatic corps went for it, slotting me for the oral exam and final round in January.

23

Then Nobleton rejected my book. The first reader's report had been stellar, the second reader's not very, but since the first had been so glowing and the history editor Deborah Joliet so persuaded of the work's potential, she was giving me another chance. She apologized for the rigorous review process, but if I would take the second reader's suggestions for extensive revisions then Nobleton would allow me to resubmit the book and they would send it to a third reader to break the deadlock. So I spent my days at the local college, ordering volumes from interlibrary loan and revamping the manuscript, then evenings I drove out to my writing course. One night after class I was invited for a drink by this 27-year-old lawyer with whom I'd had friendly exchanges.

"You'll never guess what I did," he said over our beers.

"Penned the great Jewish-American novel."

"Almost as good – I quit my law firm."

"You're joking."

"Dead serious. I'm going all out on this writing thing. You can't take half-measures."

Jeez man, I thought, wait till you can make a living at it.

"That's great," I said. "Real gutsy of you."

"You're the first person I'm telling and you know why? It was something you said – do you remember?"

"Not offhand."

"You wished you had put all your energy into writing instead of academe."

"I said that?"

"Damn straight. It inspired me. I want to thank you."

"You're welcome."

"To the literary life!"

"The literary life."

After the extension course I lost contact with him and sometimes wonder if he made it. I forget his name or else I'd google him. I feel a little responsible for the guy.

24

That year the NAH conference was in Washington D.C. In my cover letter for the professor jobs I followed Joe Vasquez's advice and underscored my "burgeoning interest in the rapidly expanding field of women's history" and wound up with five interviews, three fewer than New York a couple years prior, but five more than the big fat zero I got for the Chicago NAH convention during my Yalom Eldad stint. In my Chicago applications I had of course mentioned that I was at the INSTITUE FOR WOMEN'S STUDIES AND FEMALE EMPOWERMENT, but as of that point Nobleton hadn't yet bruited the term "Gender Studies," which in my Washington applications I now elevated to the status of a quasi-official anointment: "Nobleton College Press is considering my dissertation for its prestigious Gender Studies series . . ."

I reserved three nights at the Washington D.C. Sheraton, which was exorbitant, but the cheaper places in town were booked solid between Christmas and New Year's, and I was presently making good money with the California Unemployment Office. Of my five job interviews one was for a temporary non-tenure-track slot, so our talk was perfunctory, while the other four were various. The woman leading one of them was self-defensive, likely due to the smallness of the school and the fact that she didn't think the students were all that good either. She kept reminding me that you couldn't overload them with work; no problem, I thought, less work for me. A good interview was a college in Oklahoma – they seemed snowed by my pitch – but I didn't yearn with all my heart for a place where the most scintillating motto they could think up for their state license plates was "Oklahoma is OK." The fourth interview was with a sole guy who talked the whole time about his own research. To get him back on topic I showed him my *Gray Masses* books, which he riffled through, and by the time I rose to leave he still hadn't given them back. So instead of ending on a bad note by saying *Uh, like I mean, can I maybe have my books back*, I sacrificed them on the altar of professional advancement through personal abasement and went to Henshaw-Paul's stand for a replacement pair.

"Gladly," said a refined-looking brunette tending the stall. "Just so long as you don't leave your dissertation with us."

"You getting lots of those?"

"So many I've lost count."

"And here I thought Henshaw-Paul was an educational press."

"Which is why we don't publish dissertations!" she laughed.

"Yeah, who ever learned anything from a PhD thesis."

"But they don't seem to care. They just keep wanting to drop them off. That's how desperate things are."

She gave me the bulletin. There was a growing crisis in academic publishing with cutbacks in funding, the presses shrinking, some just scuttling their humanities lines altogether. It was about publishing more accessible and marketable stuff, not those arcane monographs which weren't designed to be read so much as simply prove you'd been a good little boy and done all your homework. I told her the accessible approach had been mine from the start.

"Do you have anyone interested?"

"Nobleton."

"Deborah Joliet's a powerbroker," she said. "You'll have a real leg up if she goes for your book."

"Not a leg up with Deborah if I get a great job offer?"

"The publishers are the arbiters these days. The universities don't know their own minds – they need the imprimatur of major presses. God forbid they should make a hiring or tenure decision based on simple good sense."

"Well, no matter what, I'll always be a Henshaw-Paul author. They can't take that away from me."

"Like the song says."

I went away wishing I had asked her out for a drink. She had style and seemed impressed by the Nobleton connection – or maybe I thought she had style just because she was impressed.

The next day was my last interview. The professor who conducted it had an Italian name and spoke with a slight Italian accent – otherwise his English was that of an American. He was somewhat diffident about his college, Western Mississippi, a good school with good students, not the caliber of Berkeley or UCLA, of course, most of them Mississippi or Louisiana residents, and the town, well, not exactly a cosmopolitan hub and sophisticate's dream but still very livable. The position was to replace a German historian who was retiring, but the main teaching duty in addition to modern Europe and more specifically modern Germany was a five-part humanities survey, and could I teach such a survey? Could I *not*. I'd been a teaching assistant in just such a survey at Zafiro Tech, he must have heard of it, the William J. Clayton Humanities Program, somewhat renowned in fact, from the *Epic of Gilgamesh* to *Waiting for Godot*, and I'd taught world history no less, from the Big Bang until yesterday's six o'clock news. Ha ha. Naturally the term world history takes in an awful lot of territory, he said, but there is a need for such courses, don't you agree? Positively, I agreed, a *fundamental* need. And were you to teach a humanities survey, Dr. McIlhenny, then what would be some of the books you might focus on? Dante is an absolute must, I stated, seeing as how his *Divine Comedy* forms a watershed between the Middle Ages and the modern era, a work steeped in religiosity and the medieval worldview, though written not in Latin but the vernacular and thus comprising a major step on the road to secularization, a principal hallmark of the modernization process in the past seven hundred years, if we're to believe Durkheim, at least, and then you must include Machiavelli's *The Prince*, which laid the theoretical groundwork for modern statecraft and the divorce between personal ethics and raison d'état, with the secularization process again at work, and we can't forget Castiglione's *Book of the Courtier*, which epitomized the Renaissance Man, the complete man, an ideal which has sadly been lost in our era of technocratic specialization, so there's a few books right there, just to mention the ones I know from my own studies with Daniel Bardoni . . . Oh, you've heard of Professor Bardoni? Yes, he's a brilliant scholar, an exceptionally brilliant scholar . . . No, to my great sorrow I don't speak Italian, I only read it . . . The Stanford humanities program? You mean their attempt to phase out people like Dante and Machiavelli and reconstitute the Western canon? Well, to be frank, it's not that I don't think the rest of the world has nothing to contribute to the civilization project, but American culture and society is largely a product of the Western tradition and I think it behooves us to take that tradition seriously . . .

For the return trip I took the train. I had already encountered compatriots who, upon learning that you'd seen a bit of the world outside U.S. borders, would throw off the moronic statement: *See America first – that's what I always say!* So I decided that the next time I was accused of not having witnessed my homeland, I could lay into them with my tale of watching the snowbound plains of our big beautiful country roll past from the comfort of an observation car. Highlight of the trip was Chicago, home to the University of Exceptional Brilliance, but where I avoided all things academic and capped my stay with a "Gangster Tour." We rode in a black bus and both the driver and the tour guide wore Chicago gangster outfits – *de rigueur* fedoras along with double-breasted suits and two-tone shoes – as they escorted us to all the old gangster haunts. We saw the Biograph Theatre where the FBI ambushed Dillinger, we viewed the place where Dean O'Banion got whacked in his flower shop (a mere front for his criminal operations, yet the man was quite fond of flowers and a gifted arranger) then we stopped at the site of the Valentine's Day Massacre. The garage where the killings took place had been razed, you needed your imagination, but the guide did a good job of painting the scene and then punctuated it with more of the hokey patter that had riddled his shtick:

"Alright, a lot more to see, so we're off like honey-moon pajamas!"

I loved it, right down to the toy tommy gun which the guide packed, and at the souvenir shop I bought a postcard of Al Capone and sent it to Bardoni with the single line: "I see this guy in a good state prison."

25

Apart from just reading the information materials that the diplomatic corps had sent me a month prior, the only preparation I did for the oral examination was to circle the date on my calendar and set my alarm clock early enough to make the 7 a.m. sign-in time at the testing center, where I was issued a visitor badge and then checked through security and took my seat with some dozen others in the anteroom. They were sizing each other up under cover of smalltalk while I sized them all up through some old-fashioned eavesdropping. One guy had a degree in international relations and I heard Georgetown mentioned, the fellow he spoke to was a lawyer who did *pro bono* work at the Men's Central Jail, someone else had studied public policy, another had interned at the United Nations, and one woman had just flown in from South Korea where she functioned in an advisory capacity to the U.S. armed forces. What had led me among these top 2-percenters, these well-groomed professionals living four-square meaningful lives? Sitting there I recalled how I had filled out the section *Illicit Narcotics and Alcoholic Beverages* on the SURVEY FOR DELICATE POSTS. I had cited two episodes of marijuana use in my life by explaining that in the first instance I was far more interested in the girls who were smoking it than the drug itself, and in the second case I had devoured a "spacecake" at a party only because it was the sole thing on hand to eat and I was famished after a long night of drunken revelry.

Maybe they were impressed by my lack of guile.

A tall white guy came in accompanied by a black woman with straightened hair. They split us into two groups and mine followed the woman into a room with a round table and six chairs. In front of each chair was a binder and a placecard that matched our badges. I was B2. In each corner of the room were chairs, three of which were already occupied by examiners with a clipboard on their lap and pen in hand. The woman explained that in this first exercise we would form a taskforce charged with earmarking funds to competing projects in some imaginary Third World country. We had thirty minutes to absorb the material in our binders and prepare a five-minute presentation as to why our certain project deserved a proportionate share of the very tight budget, then we had an additional half hour to reach a group consensus, and we were on the clock – the time limits would be strictly observed.

"Do the ladies and gentlemen have any questions?"

We had none.

"Then please commence your review of the materials."

She took her seat in the fourth chair while we opened our binders. My project was one of infrastructure. The fake country had no rail transport, almost no roads suitable for cars, and was thick with jungle; the only way into the interior was by machete or helicopter and no sea routes since it was landlocked. Where was I – equatorial Africa? Buried deep in the rainforest? What they needed was a couple airstrips for planes to open the place up to the outside world, then other infrastructure like paved roads and schools and courthouses would follow. I jotted some notes then put my pen down. Everyone else was still busy scribbling and no one spoke. We had been told by the woman that if anyone talked during this prep period then the whole group would fail. That seemed pretty dubious. I was tempted to test her on it. Like asking what she and the other three examiners could possibly be observing during the silent half hour, as they too were busy with their pens the whole time, maybe just writing down first impressions: *B2 finished after twenty minutes – seems unduly brash and bordering on insolent . . .*

"Time – pens down!"

The woman rose and leaned across the round table and tossed a sheet of paper into the middle of it – like a hockey face-off to see who controls the puck. It was so transparent that I let slip a contemptuous snort, not loud but audible, and across the way I saw one of the stone-faced examiners write something. Though it might not have been on my account since in the meantime one of our number had gone for the paper like Gretzky. He had a goody-two-shoes look behind aviator eyeglasses, the kind of guy you disliked on sight and just the type to seize this opportunity to demonstrate those **Initiative & Leadership** qualities underscored in the preparatory materials we'd been sent.

"So here's our budget," he announced, "and there seem to be certain financial constraints . . ."

He basically read from the paper. Then he proposed we go in a clockwise direction with someone keeping time.

"I'll keep time," I said hoping to demonstrate my ability in **Working with Others**.

I kept an eye on my watch as one person after another argued their case. Then I said my piece, extremely brief, just stating that infrastructure was the prerequisite for all else, without it there was no economic development, cultural exchange or social integration, so why not a couple low-cost airfields? Clear some jungle, lay down the tarmac, and we're good to go.

Gretzky came last. He was arguing for a cultural center. He tried to impress with his own linguistic culture and managed to confuse "flaunt" with "flout" and "consummate" with "consonant," though he did say "criterion" and not "criteria" in speaking of a singular. He wound things up:

"And so the ethnic and gender component – "

"TIME!"

It was no lie, he'd taken it all the way to five.

"Just to finish," he said giving me a look, "the benefits to women and ethnic minorities – "

"I'm afraid he's right," said the woman. "Your allotted time has expired."

Then they argued back and forth on how to divide the funds while I stayed out of it. I didn't want to over-play my hand, which I felt a good one, like being dealt a full house, so when they asked for my input I said: "I've made my case and I think it's self-evident." An awkward pause ensued. Like regardless *how* self-evident, you're still supposed to say *something*, so I humored them: "And I can only cite Stanley on the Congo when he said that without the railroad it wasn't worth a penny."

The woman gave me a hard look, like she was trying to figure out if the remark was racist, then we finally came to a consensus with a couple minutes to spare and I wasn't forced to call time again.

Part 1: complete.

Part 2: another binder, another ninety minutes, but this time everything on an individual basis. The binder was full of graphs and other quantitative material which you had to distill to two succinct pages so your overworked ambassador could wrap his mind around it. Sort of a rough-draft démarche, something he might send off to another government with his signature and not too many changes if any, so I put my head down and all those years of writing abstracts and précis finally paid off.

Part 3: solo interview. It began oddly with me alone in a tiny room, sitting in a chair that faced two empty ones, then came a knock at the door.

"Entrez!"

Striding through the door and taking their seats was a stocky Hispanic guy and the black woman for whom I seemed destined.

"Dr. McIlhenny," she said, "please tell us a little about yourself and why you wish to join the diplomatic corps."

I had no idea what they were looking for. But I recalled the watchwords **Oral Communication** and **Composure** and gave liberal interpretations to each by just coolly rattling off basic facts about myself and from there went into the academic career (my interlocutors now scribbling notes) and how I had spent time in Germany and France and other parts of Europe (no need for an itemized list, offhand allusion sufficed, the mark of a true cosmopolitan) and how living in Israel for nine months made me realize that one could enjoy life abroad in places other than Europe even though I still preferred Europe (so they wouldn't see it as an open invitation to send me to Kyrgyzstan or some other vowel-poor nation) . . .

"Thank you Dr. McIlhenny," said the woman looking up from her clipboard. "We would like you to now prepare a hypothetical scenario."

She handed me a sheet of paper and they sat there while I read it. As a member of the diplomatic corps, I had been stationed in a fictitious Arab country and the U.S. basketball team was in town for an international tournament. The team had gotten in some wild fracas at a nightspot, they were now jailed with the tournament scheduled to begin that next evening, and I was tasked with sorting things out.

"Ready."

"Please tell us how you would proceed," she said.

"First I need clarification. It isn't obvious from the description of our scenario whether the entire team is jailed or just certain members."

"Why should that matter?"

"Maybe we don't even have a problem. If it's only a handful of players, even the whole starting lineup, America could just field its bench and still win."

"I think we may infer that the entire team has been incarcerated."

"Then assuming I can't consult with the ambassador, and I need to make my own call here, then I'd just go to the jail and try and get them sprung."

In the information materials they had sent me, I thought to have read that in the oral exam it was neither necessary to possess any previous knowledge of an embassy's inner workings nor was resort to superiors an option.

In fact I remembered having definitely read this.

"It's not that easy," said the Hispanic guy. "There have been tense relations between the United States and this country for quite some time now. You can't just mosey on in and get our team free."

"Is there money at my disposal?"

"You mean for purposes of bribery?" he said.

"Cultural adaptability," I quoted from the playbook, thereby eschewing both **Judgment** and **Resourcefulness**, which didn't quite speak to the matter. "In these countries graft can be rampant."

"You've had experience of such countries?" said the woman.

"Egypt, Mexico," I said. "A couple other places."

"And you're saying that money can pave the way in these places."

"I imagine it would pave the way in most."

"Are you calling yourself a cynic, Dr. McIlhenny?"

"The so-called cynic's response is to say he's a realist."

"And as a realist do you sincerely believe that money changing hands would resolve our specific situation?"

"Wouldn't hurt to try."

"Perhaps it wouldn't hurt to consult your superior," she said. "There's a chain of command in the diplomatic corps."

Dirty pool. We both knew the guidelines.

"I said assuming I *can't* consult him."

"That was *your* assumption, Dr. McIlhenny."

"Well then, yeah, I guess I'd consult him."

"Or her."

I said nothing and looked at the guy, come on pal, get back into this one.

"And let us *assume*," she continued, "that your superior instructs you to refrain from any venal practices such as you've just described."

"So the ball's back in my court?"

Her turn to be silent.

"No pun intended."

They waited.

"In that case I'd tell the jailers that if they didn't release the team then I'd go straight to their government heads."

"And if those heads of government failed to react?" she said. "*Assuming* you would even have access to them."

This was growing tiresome.

"Then I'd play the race card."

"You'd play the what?" said the Hispanic guy finally.

"The Arab states aren't exactly known for their racial tolerance," I said. "It wouldn't look good if a mostly black basketball team was jailed merely owing to some youthful hijinks."

"Dr. McIlhenny," said my chief inquisitor, "I believe you're going on the *assumption* that the American basketball team would be mainly African-American."

"I am."

"That's a racial stereotype."

"The Dream Team was two-thirds black."

"You're referring to our representatives at the Barcelona Olympics?"

"Yes."

"That's irrelevant, Dr. McIlhenny. And you mentioned having traveled to Egypt. If I have my geography correct, then that's an Arab state."

I said her geography was impeccable.

"And Egypt, if I'm not mistaken," she said, "is a country of color."

"Sure, but not black."

"Egypt is also Africa."

"Not black Africa. They looked pretty non-black when I was there. Except for the Nubians in the south of course. I think they're one percent of the population. I had a Nubian guide. He was best of the bunch."

"So you know Africa?"

"Egypt."

"I said *Africa*, Dr. McIlhenny."

"You just got done saying Egypt was Africa."

After everyone had completed this third stage of the exam, both groups sat together and waited to be called into an adjoining room for the final results. I didn't wait long. In fact I was the first one called and the Hispanic guy and you-know-who broke the news to me. So I wasn't diplomat material, meaning I wasn't diplomatic, which I think I probably knew already.

26

Then I got the call back from Western Mississippi. They wanted me for an on-campus "interview" as they called it, though the interview would be two days and three nights, me arriving Thursday evening and leaving Sunday morning. I knew that Western Miss was in the boonies but didn't realize just how remote until I ordered my plane tickets, which had me landing in New Orleans, so the closest major airport was in another state. I emerged from the baggage pick-up area and saw a woman holding up a piece of paper with my name felt-tipped on it. I expected some splashy southern accent but her diction wasn't distinctive in any way, just bland white-bread American, though she turned out to be a specialist in Southern slave culture. We took off in her car and the two-lane blacktop rose and dipped over rolling hills.

"Would you mind terribly if we stopped at the supermarket to buy a few things?" she asked as we drove along. "For your party Saturday night."

I was the occasion for a departmental soirée. They did this with all their on-campus interviews and I was the second of three. At the supermarket I pushed the cart while she pulled bottles off the shelves, a fair amount of her purchase taken up with alcohol, as if putting in a store.

"Armistead County is a dry county," she explained. "We have to bring alcohol over the county line."

Of all the schools in all the towns in all the world . . .

We crossed the county line and she gave me a quick tour of things. You had a main drag with the university on one side and the residential district on the other. There were lots of Queen Anne houses with antimacassar fretwork and spacious verandas. The homes had bright green lawns extending to the edge of the street, no sidewalks or curbs intervening, and the streets themselves were tree-lined and shady. Swingsets and doughboy pools were visible in the backyards, which you saw into since they weren't walled or even fenced.

"Housing here is extremely affordable," she said and went on to quote some absurdly low prices. "Are you married? Any children? Well, it's a good place to *start* a family. Most of the people who live here are connected with the university in one form or another. It's not just some backwater. That's what I first thought when I came for my on-campus interview, oh, I don't want to even *think* how many years ago."

I asked where she was from.

"Cedar Rapids. I got my degree at Wisconsin. And you're from L.A.? Well, being from Los Angeles you probably realize it's not *where* you live but the intellectual environment that counts."

I didn't care for the slam on L.A. but let it go – someone from Iowa, just too easy.

"And don't you have your book out with Nobleton now?"

"They're considering it," I said.

"Under the rubric Gender Studies?"

"Yes."

"Very good."

She dropped me off at the bed & breakfast where I was staying the next three nights. A brick walk led to the front steps, there was a portico with columns, and the front door had a fan window above it. My room had green-and-white striped wallpaper and the ceiling sagged in the middle with a yellowing chandelier. I slept soundly and next morning was picked up by the head of the search committee – the same Italian historian who had interviewed me at the NAH convention – and we drove to the lecture I was giving to a group of history honor students. My thesis was that the rise of European fascism in the 1920s and 1930s was mainly fueled by fear of a communist takeover. Which wasn't quite true. Fascism might have existed without communism but not without the First World War. The returning soldiers wanted to relive the male camaraderie of the trenches, they wanted to wear uniforms and be violent for the sake of violence and for that they didn't need commies, but I sidestepped this notion since the search committee and the department head were also at the lecture and I figured it would only have confirmed what they thought they already knew.

Cynical realist that I was.

Afterward we toured the campus. The students were a jolt after Europe and Israel and even Zafiro/Bonita. They struck me as exceedingly wholesome – very vanilla, especially the girls, not like they were rife with daddy issues and other psychological hangups, not like they were dying of anorexia and too much molecular physics or Heidegger – just pudgy knees and artless faces wherever you looked. A fair proportion of the studentry was black, maybe fifteen percent, like their share in the general population, but even the black girls had that vanilla look. The guys, both black and white, tended toward beefy football-player types, and no Asians that I could see – probably all indoors studying.

27

Saturday morning I presented my dissertation research to the assembled faculty – a walk in the park since they were already sold on its genius due to the Nobleton connection – and then the party that night was at the home of department head Marjorie Riordan. She was petite, slightly heavy downstairs, but pretty in a boyish way with bobbed auburn hair. Professor Riordan was a Southern gal and, like half the faculty, a graduate of Duke.

"Can I get you something in the way of a drink?"

"What you got there?" I said pointing at her glass.

"Straight bourbon."

"Let 'er rip."

Everyone in the department spent at least some minutes talking to me and I was never left alone. They were tag-teaming me. I didn't mind. All of them were cordial and kept asking if they could freshen my glass. One guy was a classics scholar who coordinated the study-abroad program. Every year he sent groups of students on a summer jaunt through Europe where they received guided tours of the major cities. Would this not be something to consider?

"Don't know if I'm really qualified."

"Your résumé says you're conversant in French and German," he said. "Then of course your expertise in European history. It's actually an extension of teaching. Our first order of business here is pedagogy. Western

Miss started out as a Normal college with the mission of training teachers."

"What about sabbaticals?"

"Every seven years as a rule."

"No more often than that?"

"Every seventh year is the usual frequency. I take it you're asking because of your research needs?"

"That's right."

That was wrong. The fact was I didn't care playing babysitter to a bunch of raucous college kids on the loose in Europe – what I wanted to know was when I could be off on my own and rid of the pests. Before I'd even gotten the job, I was figuring out how to curtail and even flee its duties. Then there was the Korean-American guy from San Jose who was their new Asian Studies expert.

"So what are your impressions of Western Mississippi?" he probed.

"I like it. And now with a fellow Californian as prospective colleague, I like it even better."

"Think a left-coast boy like you could make the switch down here?"

"You seem to have pulled it off."

"It's an easy place to live. The weather is good, the people friendly, the other stuff you get used to."

"Like wet and dry counties?"

"And bizarre sex laws on the books."

"How bizarre?"

He mentioned a couple antiquated statutes.

"Then I'll have a lot of fun breaking them."

He laughed. "Maybe someone in Gender Studies

can get away with it. But we're not Cal Tech, in case you haven't noticed, and you've got Nobleton interested in your book. You can always write your way out of here and get a professorship at one of the more research-oriented schools."

Now I had already wangled the job, done my hard time, and had a tenure-track slot at a college that wasn't Western Miss. First they lay the school's teaching mission on you, preparing you for the massive course load you'll be carrying at this remedial outfit, then they say it's not so bad since you can "write your way out." That either meant there were no ambitious scholars here or they had failed in publishing their way to a more elevated post or they were just all devoted educators. It was confusing. I flopped on the couch with my bourbon and soon the hostess rejoined me. After bringing me that first drink of the evening we hadn't really spoken, but here she was now to chaperone me through to its denouement, the whole thing carefully choreographed.

"So you're heading home tomorrow," she said. "I do hope you've enjoyed your stay with us."

"My first on-campus interview."

"And you acquitted yourself very well."

She wasn't sitting so close that it was unduly intimate, but still close enough that for the first time I noticed all the broken capillaries in her cheeks.

"And what exactly *are* you returning to?" she asked. "It wasn't clear from your application just what your current institutional affiliation is."

"I took the year off to revise my dissertation for publication," which was true so far as it went and sounded better than living at home and collecting unemployment checks.

"It's with Nobleton College Press right now, isn't it?"

She knew it was. But they loved taking that word in their mouth – Nobleton – and it did sound better than Louisiana State University Press or the University of North Texas Press where professors on this faculty had published and neither of which had the same lofty ring.

"How do you rate your chances?" she asked.

"Fifty-fifty."

"Do let us know when they accept the book."

"And let you know if they don't?"

"That shouldn't be necessary," she smiled. "It'll be published under the rubric Gender Studies, have I understood that correctly?"

The flight back the next day was harrowing. Over the Gulf of Mexico a hellacious storm had our plane pitching and rolling and maybe even yawing – whatever yawing is – though my stomach was certainly yawing. The Southern guy seated behind me was even more scared than this lily-livered Yankee.

"Sweet Lord in heaven! Good God almighty! We're goin' down!"

Also not helping my morale was having a window seat. I stared in gruesome fascination at the lightning flashes as the wing visibly flexed in the storm. Occasionally I tore my eyes away and threw a furtive glance at the flight attendants to gauge their reactions. In dealing with the terrified passengers, they kept fixed smiles on their faces, but otherwise their expressions were uniformly stolid if not quite grim.

"Holy Christ! One more like that and the wings'll shear clean off! Oh mother of God!"

I signaled one of the stewardesses, who came swiftly.

"This gentleman behind me seems to be experiencing some anxiety," I explained. "I thought there might be something you could do for him."

She raised her eyes over the top of my seat.

"Sir, can I be of any assistance?"

"No."

"Are you sure I can't get you something?"

"No."

"Perhaps a drink? A moist towelette?"

"I'm fine, thank you."

"Just let me know if you need anything."

He was quiet for rest of the flight.

When confronted by female calm, male hysteria had been shamed into silence, a dynamic which could scarcely have escaped this Gender Studies expert.

28

The unemployment checks streamed in nonstop, but then I made a fatal error: I took the California Basic Educational Skills Test. They called it CBEST but it was more like CWORST, the thing so easy it was like they were testing for the job of village idiot.

This was the exam to qualify you for teaching in the Los Angeles public-school system.

I had taken the test since I needed something as backup next academic year if a university post didn't materialize. I could get the test behind me, have that in reserve, then apply to local schools if the situation warranted. But the problem was that after the test I promptly got an official offer from the school district as a substitute teacher and naturally had to accept it. If I didn't then I would have been out both my unemployment checks and a decent-paying gig. I could have tried keeping the job offer secret, but I figured that Los Angeles and Sacramento would be sharing their files on this fugitive, so I came clean.

I was credentialed as an "Emergency Multiple Subject" teacher, which meant I arose at six in the morning to wait and hear from schools where the teachers had called in sick and then I would head out unwashed and sleep-deprived to wherever needed, usually East Los Angeles. On arrival you found the principal's office and were escorted to the classroom by the secretary and given a lesson-plan which had just been phoned in by the sick teacher and which you were reading for the first time as the class sat waiting. Sometimes you didn't even have a lesson plan. But it hardly mattered either way since the kids took it as official occasion to goof off. After one or two days they would never see you again so why not? This made discipline a problem. The usual pattern was that after failing to get the class under control you sort of adopted their attitude and it was a game of mutual indifference till the bell rang and the next class filed in and the charade resumed. That was one way to play it. The other way was to get tough. One time at a junior high school I'd had enough and went into the ball closet and took out a volleyball.

"You see this? Next person out of line . . ."

They'd been talking amongst themselves while taking a quiz I had given and now fell silent as I returned to front of the classroom and paced back and forth monitoring their mouths. I thought I had them cowed but there's always one guy. He'd been the prime offender and of course had to test me. These types routinely sit in the back row (as I well knew, having once been that type) so when he whispered some words to his neighbor, with a sneaky little smile, I winged the ball from one corner of the classroom to the other.

SMACK!

Against the wall.

Missing his head by inches.

The kid was surprised I'd done it – though he still gave me backtalk: "You're lucky that missed."

"You too."

I went and retrieved the ball and resumed my pacing

at front of the room. But this time I was sweating. If he or any other kid talked again then I'd have to throw the ball. On target. They couldn't think I was missing on purpose. I was praying they wouldn't talk because he was right – I could be brought up on charges of assault.

They didn't talk.

Afterward I decided this was too nerve-wracking. I needed a permanent position where the kids knew they'd be seeing me on a daily basis and behave with concordant respect. So I started interviewing with grade schools and at the seventh interview Mountjoy Elementary offered me a job. Though located in East L.A., this was one of the "magnet schools," the cream of the crop, and I would be a general-subjects teacher for a third/fourth-grade combination on a provisional basis and with a starting salary of $2000 a month. There were just two stipulations. One was a commitment to "instruct in a language other than English" and the other was to take four semester units of "multicultural understanding." I said sure thing and signed. In a pinch I could have taught in German, perhaps some elementary French, leastwise at the grade-school level, and thought I'd petition to get the multicultural requirement waived due to my international experience and training as a cultural historian.

They didn't mean that.

They couldn't bring themselves to say it out loud but multicultural meant Mexican and the language other than English was *Spanish*. Except for a Filipino girl and a Vietnamese girl, my class of 25 kids was all Hispanic, the majority of whom had limited English, and how they got into a magnet school I have no idea. Serving as my interpreter was Mrs. Tsubaki. She was a wizened Japanese retiree who stood off to one side and gave simultaneous translations in a low voice or waited till I was done then gave capsule explanations of the work I had just assigned.

A Nippon-born woman translating the English-language lessons of some rookie punk into Spanish – that's en-ter-tain-ment!

Mrs. Tsubaki's services were even more in demand at my first parent-teacher conference. It was mostly mothers, not many fathers in evidence, and the moms stressed that I should be very firm with their kids since they needed a hard masculine hand. They seemed delighted to have a male at the helm for once. The Mountjoy staff was almost entirely women (I'd gone through the school catalogue and counted 78 women and 13 men including me and the principal, but a good half of those men must have had custodial positions and the like, since I only ever saw four other male teachers) and because I was so inexperienced and patently lousy, the sole way I could figure it was that for the first time in my life I was beneficiary of a little reverse discrimination – while affording some highly personal insight into the deleterious effects of "equity" hiring.

After two months I was burnt out and even falling asleep in class. The kids did their work in small groups, Mrs. Tsubaki went around lending a hand, and I would feel the drowsiness come on and take a seat at back of the classroom in anticipation of nodding off. It wasn't like everyone didn't notice. I had no clue what official paperwork needed to be done, I gave out grades on an impressionistic basis, but by delegating most things to Mrs. Tsubaki I could somehow muddle through each day impervious to the reality of the situation and my contractual obligations.

29

Around this time I got a phone call from Deborah Joliet. She had sent my manuscript to the third reader, my revisions had impressed, so she was approaching the Nobleton Board of Trustees to see if they wouldn't green-light it. This was happening tomorrow and she could give me a definitive answer that same afternoon. Would I be around to receive her call at 5 p.m. west-coast time?

"Perfect."

"Then let's keep a good thought."

That next day at Mountjoy I was less focused than ever. To beat rush-hour traffic on the Hollywood Free-way I left school early, leaving the kids in Mrs.Tsubaki's capable hands, and got home with half an hour to spare. My parents were still at work and I dipped into the liquor cabinet to pass the time. I thought about the Mississippi call a couple weeks back. It wasn't the department chair Marjorie Riordan who had called but the Italian fellow heading the search committee. He apologized for not having been in touch sooner, you know the red tape and bureaucratic complications involved, these things take time, but they had finally reached a decision.

"We would like to offer you the tenure-track post of assistant professor of history and concurrent director of the humanities program."

"Thank you, that's very flattering, but I can't accept."

"Do you have another offer?"

"No."

"If you're concerned about salary then we might have a bit of wiggle room on that one since yours will be a double appointment of sorts . . ."

An assistant professorship started at $32,000 and he explained how I might finagle a couple thousand more.

"It's not a question of pay," I said. "I'm just keeping my options open at the moment."

"Has Nobleton accepted your book?"

"Not yet."

"Then at this point your options would seem to be somewhat limited."

And his tone somewhat snarky.

"Yet," I said. "Nobleton hasn't accepted it *yet*."

Now here I was awaiting their verdict.

I stared out the window onto the porch where my old heavy bag hung from a chain. I still went a few rounds on it every so often and might do that today in case of bad news – put on the mitts and vent some frustration. It surprised me that Western Miss had offered me the post. I'd been ambivalent about the school from the start. Which in retrospect was why I'd given that spurious lecture on fascism, almost daring them to find me out, and the irony was that my indifference toward the job had both loosened me up and likely awed them with my offhand manner. I detected a certain self-loathing on their part, and my theory was that the best way to win the affections of someone filled with self-loathing was affect a cavalier style, which I'd learned with certain women, Judith chief among them, but with Nobleton I *hadn't* been cavalier, not at all, a bit smarmy if anything, damn it, hope my theory's all wet . . .

The call came through and Deborah Joliet's voice came on the line. She said the Board of Trustees had enthusiastically approved my book for publication. They were excited about its potential to reach a wide audience and the first print-run was planned at a lavish 3000 copies, cloth edition, 32 halftones, but its price still set at an affordable $24.95 for the non-academic buyer. She would put two copies of the contract in the mail today and I should countersign both copies and return one to Nobleton and keep the other for my files . . .

I barely heard the rest. The air was filled with music.

30

To stay amused and awake at Mountjoy, I slapped the kids with nicknames: Babaloo, Skeets, Hugo A-Go-Go, Durango Kid, Hula Man, King Oreo, etc. These were sometimes derivatives of their real names like "The Hipster" for Hipólito or my own pop-cultural associations like "Bad Man" for José or "Sugar" for Ray. One day during lunch I was approached by Ray and the three other boys in his reading group.

"Maestro, we want you to call us Sugar too."

"That okay with you, Sugar?"

He nodded.

"Alright, I hereby dub you Sugar Juan, Sugar Chep and Sugar Gabe – and in due respect for your esteemed forebear, Sugar Ray, I rechristen him THE ORIGINAL."

Big smiles.

They loved it.

Another way I kept myself from being bored was to stir things up – but only after Mrs. Tsubaki had left the classroom. When she was present I had the feeling that the woman was overseeing not just the kids but quite rightly *me*. She was with us for certain things like English and social studies, but subjects like geography and arithmetic were less language-dependent, so I was always content when she said sayonara. One time I was diagramming South America on the board when Renaldo raised his hand.

"Yeah, Skeets?"

He lowered his hand and said: "What?"

A couple minutes later he stuck his hand up again and I called on him and he once more lowered his hand: "What?"

I winged an eraser at him. It found its mark in a cloud of chalk and the class laughed. This eraser thing was something I did when the kids were disorderly and Tsubaki-san absent. Some of the Mexican parents said be not only tough on their boys but feel free to inflict corporal punishment if required – I guess they weren't aware of modern American educational precepts in the Year of Our Lord 1993 – so flinging an eraser seemed pretty harmless. (Who knew that being a teacher in the L.A. public-school system would give my throwing arm such a workout?) I had also decreed that the targeted kid had to bring the eraser back to me, so Skeets did this, at which point I smacked him on the head with it as payback for the *first* time he'd pulled his little stunt. His black hair was now powdered with chalk dust, this had the class roaring, and before he returned to his chair I hurled another eraser at him. BAM! He dutifully retrieved it and tried to run away from me as soon as he'd handed it back, but my lightning reflexes brought it down and whapped him on the fanny.

The class exploded.

Sitting in the front row was Babaloo, who said with a sly grin: "Maestro, should I shut the door?"

Now it was me laughing. Babaloo had observed that when things got nutty I would shut the door as a precaution against passersby witnessing our horseplay. But the door stayed open this time since the next day a policeman was visiting the classroom to talk about his profession, and I didn't want any extraordinary escalation fresh in the kids' minds and the cop getting wind of it. I had already overstepped the boundaries in a big way once before when I was at wits' end how to keep classroom discipline – it stemmed from the fact that I didn't have a set of classroom standards, no clear set of rules, I thought that through sheer force of personality I could keep everyone in line – so this one time I *put* them in line, outside against the wall of our classroom, and walked along their ranks giving them little prods with a yardstick to keep them standing erect and their eyes front.

This was against the law.

Also because I had kept them from lunch.

When school let out that day I caught hell from the vice-principal, a tiny carrot-haired woman, not sure why it was her since it seemed like an offense that would at least land you in the principal's office. Nor was I fired let alone prosecuted. And when I finally left of my own volition, just before summer break and after only ten weeks on the job, the principal himself was a real sport.

"Let me offer my sincerest congratulations," he said. "We'll make a general announcement to the entire faculty." He shook my hand, clasped my arm, and gave me a pat on the back. "We're sorry to lose you."

It was an awfully warm send-off – though I'm certain he was more relieved than anything.

My last day as teacher I taught my class to sing *Yankee Doodle Dandy* for the upcoming Fourth of July.

Then I staged a contest and first prize was won by Bad Man José and the Durango Kid, who teamed up for a stirring rendition, *I'm a chankee doodle dandy, a chankee doodle do or die . . .*

That last day a few of the kids gave me going-away cards. The nicest was from the Vietnamese girl Daisy. She was easily the smartest kid in the class and one big thing we had in common was that it seemed she was just as bored as me. In my own mind I had placed the girls off-limits – I didn't give them nicknames, only kidded with the boys – but Daisy had clearly been taking it all in and enjoying the show. In the card she had written: "For my favorite teacher so far." I liked the *so far.* It implied that my most favored pedagogue status would only endure till something better came along, which it surely must, and like I said, a smart girl that Daisy.

31

The principal had extended his congratulations because I'd wangled a second postdoc and this time in Berlin. Again it was the Stewart connection, but having an initial hardcover edition of 3000 with Nobleton didn't hurt. The Berlin fellowship had been vaguely in the works when I rejected the Western Miss job, but no sure thing, so I could have temporized with Western Miss and waited to see if Berlin panned out, yet mere *prospect* of another year in Berlin as opposed to a lifetime at some Mississippi teacher's college was enough for me to cut and run.

I thought that while heading in an easterly direction I could also improve my French. Up until then I had made the language something of a hobby, playing with it in my off hours, a smattering of French for the well-bred chap. But now I was determined to become a true polyglot and man of the world, so I scheduled three months of courses at the Alliance Française in Paris. I also wanted to revisit the Bibliothèque Nationale to bolster my comparative chapter on the French duel before submitting the final manuscript to Nobleton, so there were scholarly considerations, and even at the height of tourist season a stay in Paris could never be wrong. Sweetening the pot was that I had a French friend who offered to put me up at his grandparents' apartment house near the Bois de Boulogne, far from the sightseer madness, which also solved the problem of stiff Parisian rents and meant I could stay till October, at which point I would head to Berlin, pitch camp there for an academic year, and beyond that a blank per usual.

I got to Paris in late June and began attending classes at the advanced-beginner level. There was an Australian guy as well as two Irish girls, who were very nice and spoke French with a brogue, but I carefully avoided all three to enforce my self-imposed gag rule in terms of English speech. I had to be hard-nosed with the other pupils too since they always slipped into English, and this would shape up as the central drama of my daily visits to the Alliance: keeping my resolve and not talking English with this United Nations of studentry champing at the bit to speak the world's lingua franca.

The first person I spoke English with was Oliver. He was English himself. This was in the second month, during the intermediate course, after he had given a presentation on *escalade* (mountain climbing) and in his talk Oliver had opined that the French style of *escalade* was craven in comparison to the Englishman's brand of mountaineering. He quoted Reinhold Messner to the effect that the proliferation of pitons – the metal spikes you hammer into rock crevices and attach a rope to break potential falls – had killed the impossible. After class we walked to get some beers at a bar he knew on the Place St.-Sulpice and I asked if he really thought the French were less brave than the English.

"I do."

"Why is that?"

"I have a French friend I went climbing with several

weeks back and he positively refused to continue without the aid of pitons. There weren't any pre-installed in the rock and he was petrified. It was an easy climb, but he told me to carry on and he'd wait for me."

"You're saying that most Frenchmen would have reacted the same way."

"Just look at the past two wars – we've pulled their chestnuts out of the fire each time haven't we?"

"I guess they needed a little help."

"Like with the bloody pitons."

Oliver was my age and had short hair on the sides but thick on top like Samuel Beckett, a beak nose like him too, similarly tall and gaunt, and for all I knew he was Beckett's illegitimate son. He had a French girlfriend, was looking to get a job in Paris teaching Business English, but wanted back in London at some point to study law. We met at that St.-Sulpice bar a couple more times, then Oliver invited me to dinner at his apartment in Belleville, a working-class district in the 20th arrondissement. The courtyard was filthy and rancid with trash. I wasn't sure where his flat was. Climbing the stairwell I kept a lookout for it, on one of the landings a couple furtive Arabs stopped talking as I went past, then on the fourth floor I finally found Oliver's surname on a door. Inside he poured me a glass of Beaujolais, from the kitchen came the smell of simmering curry.

"Belleville," I said. "But not exactly une belle cour."

"Bloody wogs throw all their garbage in it. Just open their windows and dump it in the courtyard. I've spoken to them but they're animals."

Our entrée was a soupy concoction from the subcontinent, spaghetti the main course, and Oliver uncorked another bottle and recounted his trip to the Somme battlefield over the weekend. He had tramped up and down it with his walking stick while imagining British recruits going over the top when the whistles blew and not running or even trotting but formed up in waves and *marching* toward the German trenches – how else you expect them to bloody well do it when laden with seventy pounds of equipment – and the German machine-gunners now in position after having gone underground to their concrete bunkers to escape the week-long barrage designed to leave them dazed and cowering in their trenches but only turning the battlefield into a quagmire that made movement impossible and now depriving the British of the tactical element of surprise – but what kind of surprise is it when you undertake a massed frontal attack in broad daylight and the enemy trenches a *mile* away – the kind of surprise which produces 20,000 dead that first day is the kind of bloody surprise it is – and the whole thing an attempt to relieve pressure on the useless French at Verdun and whose casualties at the Somme were half those of the valiant British whose leadership may have employed bonehead tactics but no British troops ever *mutinied* as did the bloody coward French . . . and by this time Oliver's girlfriend Hélène had arrived along with a female acquaintance of hers who was also French, had dark blond hair and handsome gray eyes, and in the romantic light of the bar later on, after she and I had left together and gone for a nightcap, she struck me as bloody beautiful.

32

Her name was Gaelle. She invited me for dinner the next evening at her apartment in the rue Delambre in the heart of Montparnasse. She was an artist and interested in L.A. where the art world had its center and where she hoped to travel and paint someday. She was presently going through her "white period" and was especially proud of a certain squiggle she had recently "achieved." We talked English since she had lived in London a couple years and I was now letting my *Only-Speak-French* rule lapse by invoking my *Except-With-Sexy-Women-Who-Might-Want-To-Sleep-With-You* proviso. The squiggle bore faint resemblance to a female nude, and it was white, alright, white on white.

"I cannot prevent myself from smearing every inch of canvas with white, it is stronger than me," she explained. "But it is more than white, it is filled with all the colors underneath, nothing is lost but nothing is visible either."

"That's fairly obvious."

"It is not obvious! I *wish* I could paint as obviously as Mozart composed, an obvious painting is always a good one, but it needs so much time to get that it comes out with obviousness."

She had first started painting during her London sojourn, so I offered the thought that it wasn't Mozart but Turner or Constable who had taught her the virtue of obviousness, and she threw it back in my teeth.

"A good English painter doesn't exist! Except Bacon. But even if he lived in London he was Irish. And what I missed most in England was savoir-vivre. There is such a lack of style in that country! I know this is a typical French remark."

The next night we went to a movie; the day after, we met at the Pompidou Center to see the American photography exhibit; the following evening she had me over again, this time for a meal of cold chicken and champagne, and after the second bottle we became lovers. I was at the Alliance Française mornings and the Bibliothéque Nationale afternoons, so it was evenings when I would head to her apartment. We always spoke English, or almost always, when she got keyed up her English frayed at the edges and that's when she might shift to French, which we would also speak in the sexual aftermath when she was happy and fulfilled, but then she switched back to English and her underlying thought was clear: *Okay, you've had your half hour of French pillow talk, buster, now let's get back to some real communication if you don't mind . . .*

After a couple weeks it seemed like we should maybe leave her apartment, not to mention her bed, for a little fresh air and if only for a change of pace.

"Have you been to Barbizon?" she said. "It is where Impressionist painting began, nearby is the forest of Fontainebleau . . . No! A better idea! Would you like to visit my parents? They live in Rennes – have you been to Rennes?"

"I've never really been outside Paris."

"Then we go to Rennes!" she said exhaling smoke and grinding out her cigarette in the nightstand ashtray, the matter settled, and some days later we were at the Gare de Montparnasse and boarding the TGV to the capital of Brittany.

33

Her parents lived outside the city in a converted windmill not far from where her dad grew up. As a boy he had gazed across the pastures and farmland and seen that windmill rising above the flat landscape and said to himself: *Someday I shall make my home there.* The means to do so were procured by becoming an international merchant of forestry mulchers. Later he sold off the company to retire at fifty, but he had spent long years doing business in America, he liked Americans, so Gaelle was sure we'd get along. He was waiting at the Rennes station when we arrived, a sturdily built guy with a pipe wedged in his mouth. We got in his car and Gaelle insisted I sit up front with him. We chatted away, his English quite good, but Gaelle felt free to correct him.

"It is not *moose* but *mouth*," she said from the backseat. "A moose, c'est un élan."

"You understood me, no?" Monsieur Gasquel asked.

"Of course."

Before long the windmill loomed up, now minus its blades, and Monsieur Gasquel began recounting the story of an ambitious young man whose imagination had tilted at the thing by dreaming the impossible dream of someday setting up residence there . . .

"I already told him, Papa," said Gaelle.

"Why not hear it again? Americans enjoy success stories, local boy makes good, is that not the phrase?"

He gave me a wink. "And my daughter shall possess it when my wife and I are deceased – though she must promise not to sell it."

"I will not sell it, but the agence immobilière."

"She jokes."

We drove up the gravel driveway. Standing at its end was the mother and the family dog. Madame Gasquel was thin and bird-like, her first name Lanette, the dog a low-slung creature of waddling gait whose name was Vivienne.

"Dis bonjour à Steve!" said Madame Gasquel to the dog.

I bent and rubbed her head and she yipped in some kind of appreciation.

"Tha's Veev-yen-uh," said Monsieur Gasquel.

They showed us to the guesthouse. It was a kitchen with bar, other side of the bar was a livingroom, and in the livingroom's corner was a queen-size bed. Off from the kitchen was a bathroom and upstairs a bedroom and another WC. We deposited our travel bags and went to lunch. First came the appetizers, which were anchovies on pieces of toasted bread, then we had salade niçoise with a dry red wine. We sat under a blue-and-white umbrella at one end of their long glittering pool. Monsieur Gasquel had a nice spread – it seemed like something to aspire to – a man of leisure and lord of your manor. Sole problem was that I disliked the notion of selling forestry mulchers for thirty years to arrive at this point. The parents were speaking English to me and Gaelle protested that I understood French perfectly.

"Steve," said Monsieur Gasquel taking up her gambit, "le vin, c'est bon, non?"

"Le vin, c'est super – un peu plus, s'il vous plaît."

"Steve, have you enjoyed your stay in France so far?" asked Lanette, also in French, and serving up this standard and clearly articulated question as if she were a teacher at the Alliance Française drilling the *passé composé*.

"Very much."

"You don't miss America?"

"Not at all."

"Steve is not a true American," stated Gaelle confidently. "He appreciates the finer things – he pursues the life of the mind."

"Not only," I said. "I like surfing, other non-mind stuff."

"But you are an intellectual, no?" said Monsieur Gasquel. "I imagine it would be very hard to be an intellectual in America. You are always fighting against John Wayne."

"Wouldn't want to take on the Duke," I said keeping things French by employing *le duc*.

"He was a duke?" said Madame Gasquel.

"Not a duke," said Gaelle. "But I heard that John Wayne was homosexual."

"John Wayne wasn't homosexual," I said.

"Oh yes, he had an affair with Truman Capote."

"Where'd you hear that?"

"We don't want to insult America's national hero," said Monsieur Gasquel.

The main course was chicken basted in something

delicious and garnished with sautéed potatoes and heaps of bread to mop it up. Bees arrived on the scene. It was getting hot. Instead of protecting us from the sun, the taut canvas above our heads seemed only to refract and intensify the rays.

"So Steve," said Madame Gasquel, "how do French girls compare to American girls?"

"*Maman!*" remonstrated Gaelle.

"It is not a fair question, Lanette," said Monsieur Gasquel.

"It is very fair," she said. "He is an American man in France and no homosexual like John Wayne."

"He wasn't homosexual, Lanette," said Monsieur Gasquel.

"I read it in *Paris Match*," said Gaelle.

"I prefer French girls," I said. "They know so much about John Wayne."

"He doesn't want to answer," said Gaelle.

"And German women?" pursued Lanette. "Gaelle tells us you have spent much time in Germany."

Gaelle's fork clattered to her plate. "*Mamaaaaan!*"

"I like German women better than American women too."

"And better than Frenchwomen?"

"Never better than Frenchwomen."

"But the Germans have very beautiful women," said Madame Gasquel. "Marlene Dietrich, Romy Schneider, Claudia Schiffer . . ."

"I once saw Claudia Schiffer on a flight to Chicago," weighed in Monsieur Gasquel and pronouncing it *Shee*-ca-go. "She was waiting for the toilet. I walked by and she smiled at me and her teeth were much too big."

"*Mais nooooooooon!*" said Gaelle. "Her teeth are too small!"

"I saw them," said Monsieur Gasquel. "They were like those of the wolf in *Le Petit Chaperon Rouge*."

"But Papa, she is a very tall woman and tall women require tall teeth to appear balanced. I tell you, her teeth are much too short for her height."

"And I tell you, I saw them as close as I am to you now, and they were like the keys of a piano."

"Black ones too?" I quipped.

"Big white teeth," he said. "Very white. Too white."

"And that is why you had the impression that they were large," said Gaelle. "Very white teeth seem much bigger than they are. I swear to you, for a person her size, her teeth are much too short."

Well, of course Gaelle knew her white. We concluded with a tarte aux pommes that I was conferred the honor of cutting, then Monsieur Gasquel broke out a liqueur, something from the roots of some plant found in the mountains somewhere in France, which had virtually no alcohol taste, and I had a refill or two then retired to the bungalow for a nap.

34

Gaelle was beside me when I woke. She hadn't originally gone to nap with me, but here she was now and still sleeping. Her bare shoulders issued from the covers, a luscious brown against the white counterpane, like some creative French dessert of caramel jacketed in angel food. She was facing away from me and I moved up against her and lightly kissed her shoulder.

"Gaelle? You awake?"

She stirred and sighed, snuggling her bottom into my lap.

"Is that a yes or no?"

"Mmmm."

I reached around and drew her against my body as her bottom continued its snuggling action. I nuzzled her neck and stroked her hip. She turned her head and we began deep kissing, soon she was on her back with me sliding in and out, when a loud buzzing came from the wall near our bed.

"What's that?"

"The telephone."

"Telephone?"

"From the house."

"Ignore it!"

The buzzing continued. It was so loud and insistent that the vibrations sent the receiver plunging to the floor. Gaelle laughed: "I don't think we *can* ignore it."

I jumped out of bed and picked up the receiver.

"Allô?"

"Steven," came Lanette's voice, "c'est l'heure du dîner."

"Oui?"

"Oui."

I replaced the phone (it had some weak magnetic attachment in place of a cradle) then struggled back into my clothes while emitting groans of self-pity.

"Is it dinnertime *already*?"

"You don't know how long you slept," said Gaelle. "You had much alcohol."

"I was tired from the trip – and all that food – very good but a bit heavy for lunch."

"Lunch is our first big meal of the day in France. We don't eat enormous American breakfasts."

I finished tying my shoes and sat on the side of the bed waiting for Gaelle to finish combing her hair. I reached up and took my jaw in hand and moved it gingerly back and forth.

"My moose is still tired from chewing."

"Then be quiet – you will only make it more tired by speaking."

The first course was salmon on pancakes with lemon juice and the wine a chilled Alsatian Riesling. Monsieur Gasquel did a good job of filling my glass, ending with a little upward twist of his wrist to cleanly break off the flow from the long-necked bottle. The evening was almost as hot as the day and the cicadas were chirping like crazy. The second course was steak with slices of cooked mushrooms, nothing else on the steak, no salt or pepper, the pure meat juices coming through, and we switched to Châteauneuf-du-Pape for that. After we polished off the steak, Madame Gasquel brought out the cheese. There was a whole platter to choose from, including a black one called chèvre cendré and seven or eight varieties all told, but I played it safe with the one I knew.

"Steve, vous aimez le camembert fort?"

I pointed antically at my stuffed cheeks. I'd been able to follow Gaelle's advice about not speaking because my mouth had been full from the start. Then after a dessert of brutally rich fudge, we climbed the stairs to the mill's third floor and took seats in a windowed alcove that overlooked the pool, which glowed electric blue through the night. In the alcove was a dainty carved-wood table where Monsieur Gasquel placed the carafe of cognac. The women sipped something called crème de framboise.

"Vous êtes professeur d'histoire à l'université?" asked Monsieur Gasquel refilling our glasses.

"Pas exactement," I said. "I taught some courses a couple years back but no permanent position."

"Nobleton College Press will publish his dissertation," Gaelle said, Monsieur Gasquel asked what my dissertation was about, and I gave them a mercifully brief explanation – merciful on my French.

"And this was your thèse de doctorat?" said Lanette.

"His PhD," said Gaelle. "He is a doctor of philosophy."

"But you did not write on philosophy," said Lanette.

"It's the American expression," said Monsieur Gasquel.

"When one writes on history?" said Lanette.

"Steve of course knows philosophy," said Gaelle.

"Who is your favorite philosopher?" Lanette asked me.

"Friedrich Nietzsche."

"Ah, Nietzsche," said Monsieur Gasquel pronouncing it the French way *Neech*. "His favorite composer was Bizet."

"Do you know Neech?" I asked.

"I read him when I was young: *Par-delà le bien et le mal*. I enjoyed his views on women."

"And they were?" asked Lanette.

"He mistrusted them," said Monsieur Gasquel.

"All philosophers are misogynists," said Gaelle.

"All philosophers are misogynists because all philosophers are men," said Monsieur Gasquel.

"You say that all men are misogynists," said Gaelle.

"Just the philosophers – only those who have thought deeply on the subject. Is it not true, Steven?"

"Not many of them married, that's a fact."

"What woman would want to marry Neech," said Gaelle. "And kiss that disgusting moostache."

"Ah, my doe, not all of them are so bad," said Monsieur Gasquel. "Camus for instance."

"Camus was a writer, not a philosopher," said Gaelle. "Sartre was the philosopher and he was an ugly little gnome."

"Simone de Beauvoir was a beauty when younger," said Lanette. "He was not too ugly for her – or for many women."

"But still ugly," said Gaelle.

"Rousseau was handsome as a young man," said Monsieur Gasquel. "And Charles Fourier."

"Fourier was a feminist," I said.

"C'est vrai?" said Monsieur Gasquel, the validity of his bold thesis now hanging in the balance.

"But not a philosopher," I added. "At least not a credible one. He thought humans would eventually grow tails."

"The men may yet," said Lanette.

"So you know the French thinkers," said Monsieur Gasquel. "Do you know the French historians? Marc Bloch? His work on the Middle Ages?"

"The *Annales* school."

"And Georges Duby?"

"Though I've never read him."

"You have not read Duby? I have a video narrated by Duby on French cathedrals. Would you like to watch it?"

"Mais Papa, non!"

"Well, perhaps you would not like to watch it."

"Of course I'd like to watch it."

"It is not long, just an hour. Will the ladies be joining us? No? Very well, come."

35

The next morning, except for that corner of the room where I now lay in bed, the bungalow was suffused in sunlight. Gaelle was sitting dressed in the breakfast nook with a coffee mug and cigarette. She smiled at me as I stretched myself awake.

"How did you sleep?"

"Not bad," I said. "And you?"

"Not bad."

"I didn't wake you when I came in last night?"

"You didn't wake me. Did my father bore you with his cathedrals?"

"I'm afraid I bored him with my lack of anything terribly bright to say on the subject."

"He is only bored when he cannot be the authority. Because you had nothing to say, he probably thinks you are a highly cultivated and intelligent man."

"Fooled him."

"You are intelligent," she said stirring a spoon in her mug. "But perhaps we should speak of the cultivated part. You cannot remember what you did last night?"

"Last night? What I did? You mean an uncultivated thing?"

She kept stirring the coffee while raising her eyebrows and turning down the corners of her mouth as if to express: *It is you who say this, mon cher, not I.*

"When I used the wrong spoon for the fudge?"

"That was not good, but understandable."

"I didn't ask for ketchup did I?"

"Fortunately no."

"Then tell me, we could be here all morning guessing. I mean, I must have committed any number of faux pas and breaches of etiquette since we got off the train."

"You really don't remember? You were that drunk? Then I will tell you – you served yourself from the cognac."

I recalled that moment to mind. Yes, I had served myself from the cognac.

"I served your father as well."

"It is not your place to serve anyone, you are not the host."

"The carafe was in the middle of the table – equidistant between us – for me that's a sign I can serve."

"Not in France."

"And in case you didn't notice, I filled his glass first and only *then* filled mine. It was an act of male bonding – here's to ya, pal, here's spit in your eye. And he didn't seem to object."

"My father is a gentleman, he would never show his displeasure."

"And we got on like gangbusters afterward. In fact you know what – I believe I may have done it *again*. What do you think of that? Twice in one evening."

"It would not surprise me. But it would have been the third time that day. Over lunch you asked for more wine."

"So did you."

"But it is *my* family and you are the *guest* and this was our *first* meal together. Perhaps on our final day together, if we get on like bang-gusters, then you can ask for more wine – but even then it would be exceptional."

"Anything else?"

"Today is my mother's birthday and we are visiting an elegant restaurant."

"If I'd known, I would have brought a present."

"Please make a present of your manners."

In the run-up to dinner we had another extravagant lunch. It dragged on two hours, from the beef bourguignon with an anomalous cherry on top through to the last excruciating piece of mimolette cheese, but I was on my best behavior and didn't once ask for a wine refill. At the restaurant that evening we all dined on eel, frog legs and escargot. I think they ordered these latter two for my benefit – classic French cuisine – but I noticed little taste with the frog legs and absolutely none with the snails, which were so small that you had a utensil the size of tweezers to prize them from their shells, then after dipping them in the warm butter that's all you tasted: warm butter. The frog legs tasted faintly of meat, but it was such a tedious operation to separate the flesh from the leg bones and cartilage – and there had been so much buildup in your mind over the years about what a marvelous *haute cuisine* frog legs were – that by the time you inserted the micro-sliver of flesh into your mouth it was one of life's greater disappointments.

36

Next afternoon I rode to the local village with Monsieur Gasquel to buy seafood while Gaelle drove into Rennes with her mother to get a haircut and run errands. That was no fun for a man, she said, the implication being that I should partake of more virile activity and go shopping for dinner. The store we visited had a counter enclosed in glass with the seafood on ice. The crabs were stacked on top of each other like a group-sex tableau dreamed up by the Marquis de Sade. The salmon had their decapitated heads placed at the tail-end of their bodies like the noggins of guillotine victims on display for the sans-culottes. Monsieur Gasquel picked out what he thought were choice specimens, particularly among the shellfish, then we carried them out to the ice chest in back of his car.

"Shall we have a drink?" he asked, our labors complete.

We walked along narrow streets with sidewalks so slim you had to go single file. At the bar we ordered two *demis*. I took tiny sips. I wasn't feeling so hot.

"Could be the snails," said Monsieur Gasquel.

"You look in fine shape."

"I am of course used to them."

I drained off my beer, he ordered two more, and when they came he said: "Gaelle wishes to go to Los Angeles. She says it is the only city in the world where one can paint. Paris is over, London is impossible, New York . . .

I forget what she says about New York. Is Los Angeles a good city for painting? Has it many great painters?"

I tried to think of great L.A. painters.

"David Hockney," I said though he was one of those execrable English. "The guy who paints the swimming pools."

"I ask myself what Gaelle will paint."

"Not swimming pools – swimming pools are blue and she's in her white phase."

"What is white in Los Angeles?"

"Not much these days."

"It is important that she have something to paint because she wishes to receive her *héritage* – how do you say that in English?"

"Inheritance."

"She asked me last night for her inheritance."

This was all news to me: inheritance, quitting her job, the imminent move to L.A. The evening before, after our dinner at the restaurant, I had gone to bed alone since Gaelle had stayed up with her father in the windmill and that's when they must have discussed it . . .

"Am I indiscreet?" he said. "It is my money. I can speak of it as I wish. Would you like another beer?"

We had one more round then drove back to the windmill.

37

That evening was a repeat of the restaurant. We spent as much time manipulating our food as eating it – cracking lobster claws, snapping crayfish, bashing in crabs, and picking out the meat of diverse other crustaceans with our slime-covered fingers. My queasiness of the afternoon had meantime transformed into full-blown diarrhea and my bowel was having more movements than a Mahler symphony. In between bathroom visits I picked at my lobster and sipped white wine, a Sancerre, which made me feel slightly better.

"It is because you are dehydrated," said Monsieur Gasquel. "You need fluids."

He was taking a mallet to something in a purple shell.

"Perhaps he is dehydrated with all the beer he drank this afternoon," said Gaelle.

"We did not drink much beer," said Monsieur Gasquel. "Would you like more wine?"

"Bien sûr," I said.

At meal's end he broke out the cognac. We got into a discussion about its purest form since this certain bottle had a number of select liqueurs blended with it, and the liqueurs were a secret recipe it was given only a privileged few to know. Actually this first bottle of cognac, which he hadn't yet poured, was for sheer purpose of comparison since then came the *other* bottle, the pure stuff, 70 percent by volume. Monsieur Gasquel gave me a shot glass of the cognac and a shot glass of the pure stuff and both went down the hatch. Gaelle observed the debauched proceedings with supreme indulgence. Then it was discovered a mistake had been made – this wasn't the *real* pure stuff! After a renewed trip to the liquor cabinet, Monsieur Gasquel placed a shot glass of this rare elixir before me, which I gulped down like a champ.

I'd never drunk nitroglycerine before.

I felt the explosion coming on and raced to the bathroom. In the past two hours I had grown well acquainted with the place, and Gaelle herself might have conceived the color scheme: white tiles, white-painted walls and ceiling, white cupboards, white bathtub, white shower curtain, white towels on stainless-steel racks, and that old standby white toilet paper. I was once more enthroned on the white toilet seat when I felt my dinner coming up and did a quick about-face, just in time, and while spewing vomit my sphincter muscle unclenched.

Did I fail to mention the fluffy white rug engirdling the base of the toilet?

There was more vomiting to do. When I finally concluded, it felt like I had performed a thousand stomach crunches.

"Steven? Ça va?"

Madame Gasquel.

"Oui, ça va, seulement un peu de vomite."

I didn't know the French word but she got the picture.

"Oh la la."

She shouted into the dining room: "Steven a vomi!"

This followed by the just audible sound of Gaelle groaning: "Merde!"

Exactly.

"Alors, vous allez mieux maintenant?" asked Madame Gasquel through the closed door.

"Oui, beaucoup mieux. Je reste ici un petit peu de temps dans le cas que ce n'est pas fini. Je crois que non."

"C'est vrai?"

"Malheureusement."

"Nous vous attendrons."

It had spattered everywhere except the ceiling. I used a couple rolls of toilet paper in restoring things to their immaculate state, but it wasn't easy cleaning the cracks between the tiles, which required some scrubbing with the toilet brush.

"Steve!" Monsieur Gasquel. "You are okay? What are you doing?"

I had the water running in the bath and was doing my damnedest to expunge the brown vestiges from the white tootsie rug. I should have done it straight-away, since the fecal matter had too much time to be absorbed by the fleecy material, so I was using the toilet brush here now too.

"I'm taking a shower!" I answered. "I got vomit all over me, just cleaning myself up!"

"D'accord. We will keep the food on the table if you are still hungry."

Mon Dieu.

The stains were stubborn – but my desperation was far greater than those stains were stubborn. A little stray barf having splattered would have been understandable, but that a grown man should have completely missed the pot while taking a *crap* seemed beyond normal human credulity. I examined my progress. Not every last splotch had been laundered from the tootsie rug, tufts of the white fabric remained tipped with it like the browned meringue on a baked Alaska, but maybe they would think it was Vivienne. Was she incontinent, that little waddling sausage?

Then I applied the hand soap to the rug, which finally did the trick.

I was in the bathroom nearly an hour, and when at last I emerged Gaelle had returned to the bungalow. I begged off any more food, said a sheepish good night to Monsieur and Madame Gasquel, then walked outside taking deep breaths of the night air to brace myself for whatever might await. But she wasn't in bed. I walked softly up the carpet-covered steps to the upstairs bedroom and found the door shut. I walked back down, gave my teeth a good brushing, then went to sleep more or less.

38

I woke to the clatter of dishes. I lay in bed listening to water running in the sink, the clash of silverware, the stacking of plates. I gauged how I felt. Not great, not like a world-beater, but no pressing need to hit the head. I kicked off the covers and went over to the bar separating the kitchen area from the livingroom and took a seat on one of the stools. Might as well get it over with.

"Did I wake you?" said Gaelle sweetly. "I tried to be as quiet as possible."

"No, you didn't wake me, my internal alarm clock just happened to go off when you slammed that cupboard door."

"I'm glad."

She banged around some more.

"And you?" I asked. "Sleep well?"

"Exquisitely."

"Bed up there pretty comfortable?"

"Like a cloud," shooting me a bright smile as she wiped around the sink.

"I got in a little later."

"You mean you didn't sleep in the bathtub of my parents?"

"Not very cloudlike."

She finished her wiping and threaded the dishtowel through a drawer handle. "I wish to speak to you."

"Aren't we doing that?"

She went to her pack of Gauloises bleues and lit one.

I spun round on my barstool and followed her movements as she continued to the livingroom and slouched into one of the easychairs. She sat with her legs crossed and elbows poised on the armrests, her fingertips touching and the cigarette between her digits trailing smoke like the chimney on a peaked-roof house. She remained in that pose, staring into space, taking a couple languid puffs and showing her ballerina neck as she blew the smoke upward.

"I am very disgusted with you."

"I gathered that."

"It is not only last night and your drinking – you are completely unaware of your surroundings. Almost everything I just now cleaned in the kitchen was your mess. Your beer bottles, your dishes, your crumbs of bread. And each time you take a shower you hang your towel incorrectly to dry. I must hang it correctly for you. I am not your mother."

I had drunk two more beers out by the pool the day before and then brought them into the bungalow, not wanting to bother her parents with my trash. There was a garbage can in the kitchen, but I had placed the bottles on the counter since I wasn't sure if there was some kind of special receptacle for glass. The Europeans were picky about these things and I hadn't got around to asking Gaelle for any specifics on the Dark-Glass-Beer-Bottle disposal issue. The other stuff she was right about.

"You have no consideration for others," she said. "You are obstinate and arrogant. You are unable to live a shared life – une vie partagée – because you are a self-centered egoist who thinks only of himself and never of others. I am an elegant woman. I could not imagine living with you for more than one week."

"That's optimistic – so far it's been only three days."

"And your behavior at this moment is rustic and brutal."

She pronounced these words with accent on the second syllables – rus*teec* and bru*tal* – not that it changed their real or intended meanings.

"Finished?"

"For now."

"Because sometimes I ask myself what an elegant woman like you is doing with a rustic brute like me. I really wonder. Or maybe I don't. Is it because I'm from L.A.? Is that the attraction? In fact I think your wanting me on my best behavior with your parents this trip is because you wanted to ask your father for your inheritance. Yeah, he told me about it, and that you're heading to Los Angeles. I mean, hey, we're all independent parties here and can do what we want, there's no king anymore in France, but I kind of wish that I'd been informed."

She took a calm puff.

"Steven, it is *you* who are going to another city, another country. There was never a moment in the past six weeks when you spoke of us, it was always *your* year in Berlin and *your* future plans, but never in Paris and never together. So I am making my own plans. If you wish to accompany me, you are invited. But would you invite me to go to with you? Wherever that might be? And I would go. I would go in a second."

There were tears on her cheeks.

"I'll send for you," I said. "As soon as I get a position. As soon as I get established somewhere."

"You won't. And I don't ask you. But what I ask you is *please* do not reproach me for leading my own life."

"Berlin's not far away."

"It is far away – as far as we are from each other now."

"You see, not far at all," I said with a weak smile.

No reply. I went over and sat on the arm of the chair and took her hand. "Hey, I didn't expect this."

"Of course you didn't expect!" and yanking back her hand. "You expected nothing from us! Only your pleasure! Nothing except I would behave myself like a good little French girl!"

"Gaelle."

"I tell you! Of course you didn't know! You concern only with yourself! That is something you would never see!"

"I have feelings for you too."

"No!"

"I do."

"I don't want to hear!"

"Berlin is just a year and then I'm up for grabs. Who knows where I'll be after that? Life can take some crazy turns. We just have to be patient and see how things develop – "

"Oh shut your moose!"

39

On the train Gaelle and I made up a little and on arrival at the Gare de Montparnasse we were friendly again – so friendly that she invited me to spend the rest of the day and evening with her. Much of this time was taken up in discussion of how things stood between us, though it was mostly just a rehash of what had been broached that morning. She tried to clarify her outburst by explaining that she was hypersensitive to any violation of her living space, that she had been concerned for some time now with my lack of fastidiousness, that the long weekend was just the culmination of this.

As for her L.A. plans, they were on hold.

That evening at dinner I was very circumspect. I allowed myself some wine, but only two glasses, then insisted on doing the dishes to which she assented with no caustic asides. *At least he's making an effort – let's not discourage him.* At one point that afternoon we had taken a nap together on the bed – nothing beyond this – and afterward I took the initiative of remaking it and smoothing out the bedspread, just so, and was generally extra careful. *Maybe he's learning.* However, late that night I did succeed in spilling some bottled water on her hardwood floor as I groped for it on my side of the bed, next morning I saw that it had left a discoloration which I tried to covertly scrub out, but it was even more resistant than the shit stains the evening before, so I hoped it might fade with time, though doubted it would, yet it was on that side of the bed which she didn't sleep on, the side close to the wall, so perhaps she wouldn't see it, at least very soon, and before leaving I made sure to hang my towel right.

A week later, the day before I headed to Berlin, I saw Oliver one last time. We rendezvoused at the St.-Sulpice bar where we had gone our first meeting. Still looking like a young Samuel Beckett, he now and then chatted French with the bartender while employing a deliberately horrible English accent. We drank several *demis* then set off for the Seine to watch a crew race. It was a French team versus an English one. The English boat wasn't that good, or just not in training, since they got trounced by the French and were several lengths back as they passed beneath us on the Pont d'Austerlitz. Oliver cupped his hands and bellowed: "BLAME IT ON THE CROISSANTS!"

40

My address for the next year was an academic institute housed in a turn-of-the-century villa in Berlin's extreme west, one of the city's tonier neighborhoods, and at edge of a forest where most of the duels had taken place and where wild boar still roamed. My workspace was on the first floor in an oval room with a high molded ceiling and creaky hardwood floor. It had once been the villa's conservatory but now had a long conference table through its center and the surrounding walls lined with gray metal bookcases. At one end of the room were windows and emplaced before them were two cast-iron desks, each with a computer, one of them mine and the other that of a colleague. It was understood that my time would be spent in preparing the dueling book for publication, but my official make-work "job" was to write up a study which would prep my boss for a three-day symposium the institute was hosting that spring. His office was at opposite end of the room behind two oaken sliding doors that met in the middle under a squared-off arch. You heard the doors rumble open and looked up and he might or might not be coming your way in his V-neck sweater and baggy corduroy trousers and designer-frame glasses. He not only ran this place but was finishing up his habilitation, which was basically a second PhD dissertation. You couldn't become a full professor of history in Germany without one. It involved years of intensive research and was monitored and reviewed and then defended before a committee – just as with the dissertation. I couldn't imagine doing two of these things in one lifetime, let alone back-to-back. It was cruel and unusual punishment, with origins in the seventeenth century, and had only survived into modern times since those presently holding professorships didn't want scholars coming up through the ranks to suffer any less than they had. The habilitation of my boss was some monumental study on the marriage and residence patterns of peripatetic sawmill workers in nineteenth-century Switzerland, Germany and Austria-Hungary, and he was pushing fifty years of age so had to get this thing done and out or else miss the boat for that much cherished professor job. He was a smoker, you rarely saw him without a cigarette, and when the guy wasn't puffing away he was taut as a wire and his head had a palsy-like tremble. He seemed to be cracking under the strain. Other than that, his theoretical paradigm was Max Weber's thousand-page *Wirtschaft und Gesellschaft*, a strain that would have me cracking all by itself.

The place's name was the Institute for Modern Comparative History, and I had qualified for the fellowship based on my ethnological chapter contrasting the French and German duels. The institute purported to do comparative history on topics which I found brain-numbing – public health in North America and Europe, agrarian policy in Turkey and Russia, infant mortality in Reykjavík and Singapore – but the one thing which was a subject of fascination to not just German historians but people the world over was strangely off limits to any comparison: the Third Reich and the Holocaust. I tried addressing the issue with the other postdocs, all of them German, but you couldn't mention Stalin or Pol Pot or Mao in the same breath with Hitler since fascist violence trumped communist violence every time. The commies got a pass not only because Marxism was a so-called scientific theory that served as an all-encompassing explanatory model for the world's social ills (my postdoc colleagues got quasi-orgasmic if they could mention these, their favorite words, in the same breath: *theory, social* and *explanatory model*) but the Marxists were high-minded and striving for world peace and a social utopia, and if millions of Ukrainians bit the dust (literally: sometimes eating dirt during the Great Famine) it was regrettable and an unfortunate perversion of "true" communism, but the poor luckless bastards were just on the wrong side of history. All these postdocs were German but they were *West* Germans, meaning no East Germans who had lived under Russian occupation and communist rule, and I wondered how they might have felt about things. But these *Wessis* were careerists all and wished no suspicion cast that they were allowing the Nazis and their crimes to be *relativiert* ("relativized": their buzzword for whitewashed) so you had the absurd situation of comparative historians at the Institute for Modern Comparative History being unwilling to compare pivotal events of the modern era.

I wasn't sure what was more impressive – the moral cowardice or intellectual dishonesty.

One time I had it out with another postdoc. He laid the Holocaust-As-Unparalleled-Crime-Against-Humanity trip on me and added that an American could have no idea how ashamed he was to be German. I cited our enslavement of blacks, our decimation of the Indians, but he didn't want to hear it. Then I tried him on Vietnam, how we napalmed it to kingdom come, and declared that if push came to shove I'd rather be gassed than burnt to a crisp.

"You're excusing Auschwitz!"

"By comparing it to Vietnam?"

"VIETNAM WASN'T SYSTEMATIC GENOCIDE!"

And that seemed to settle it. Germans couldn't help throwing the word "systematic" into the equation, which evidently made it a far greater evil than just random or even targeted but less-than-efficient murder, and who was more systematic than the Germans? My favorite quote on this was from the Austrian writer Robert Musil, who said that Germans don't know whether they want heaven or hell but only know they want to organize it. I was aching to cite that one in our discussions, but it would have only dumped napalm on their self-immo-lating fire. There seemed a freakish pride at work in the Germans – like they *enjoyed* being the world's archvil-lains – and though of course you couldn't blame them, the Jews were inadvertent shills by making a holy historic shrine to the Shoa.

It was a snarled psycho-historical complex, and at a certain point I stopped caring and let them have their little pleasure.

I was having few pleasures myself, particularly of a carnal nature. The female postdocs at the institute were uniformly asexual, neither physically appetizing nor fun, just mannish intellectuals who seemed determined that you be equally glum in their presence and hated your guts if you hadn't memorized Adorno's *Minima Moralia* in the original German. The closest I'd gotten to meeting potentially genial women had been for about eight seconds in an exchange I had with another guy at the institute.

"Some friends of mine get together once a week for an evening of polka," he said. "You might like to join us."

I had danced polka a couple times in my life, at beer gardens, an easy dance – step-hop, step-hop . . .

"I don't have a partner," I said. "You got any extra girls?"

He looked at me strangely. "We don't want girls, it's better all guys."

"Really?"

"Girls ruin the atmosphere."

"And what atmosphere is that?"

"Guys with guys," he said plainly. "Girls are just a distraction."

I'd never judged this dude a *Schwuchtel*, but hey, Berlin wasn't exactly Bible Belt territory.

"And where do you have these polka evenings?"

"We rotate," he said. "This week it's at my place."

"You must have a big place."

"How big a place you need to play polka?"

That's when I heard it: *poker*. The verb "play" tipped me off. He'd been talking poker the whole time, but the way Germans pronounce the word it comes out *pokah*. So that next night we played, and it wasn't strip poker, a thought which had also crossed my mind.

41

I'd been to San Francisco on a couple prior occasions but had never flown in, and eleven hours out of Frankfurt my plane swung out briefly over the Pacific Ocean then turned back toward the mainland and dove for the runway. We seemed perilously close to the water – I could see the tiny air bladders on the clumps of brown kelp – then out of nowhere came the landing strip and suddenly we were on it with barely time to get scared. I was in town for the annual NAH conference, which was scary enough, and this time as part of a panel on dueling, which would look good on my résumé, though the old résumé hadn't done me much good this time around with just three interviews. They were getting less each year as my qualifications mounted. After giving my panel-paper in the Hilton's Michelangelo Room – the paper itself no work of art, but the audience seemed to like it – I met with Stewart in the hotel bar.

"I only permit myself this stuff once a month, goes straight to the gut," he said taking a hit off his scotch. "So how were your interviews?"

"Clutterbuck College stood me up twice. When we finally got together the third time, one of the two interviewers left halfway through since she had important business to attend to."

"Like your interview wasn't important."

"Right."

"I think you should cross them off your list."

"I'm sure they've beaten me to it."

"And your next interview?"

"Lowderhatch University."

"Another institution with which I'm sadly unfamiliar."

"They had me promise to foot half the bill for a round-trip transatlantic flight if they gave me an on-campus interview."

"That's unconscionable."

"I consider myself lucky. When I was in Yalom Eldad I didn't get a single invite to the Chicago NAH congress. I figured it was for that very reason: restricted budgets."

"And why the market's so slow – though hardly impenetrable, three interviews this time."

"Only because of the Nobleton contract."

"Or the critical mass of your CV. But I'll admit the situation for young white males is dreadful. If only you were a woman – preferably black and lesbian. Our candidates scarcely have a chance unless they're freaks or superstars."

"And I'm just a star."

We sat over our drinks.

"Of course you could have had the Mississippi job."

"Vernon, would you have taken that job?"

"Perhaps not."

He seemed genuinely perplexed. Back in his day everything had been a snap. A snap getting into the Ivy League, a snap getting his Rhodes scholarship, a snap getting the Zafiro job, a snap getting published by Nobleton, for that matter, straight from his dissertation into print.

"You spoke of three interviews," he said. "What was the third?"

I named a certain southern evangelical college.

"I'm sure they're not beating the bushes for black lesbians."

"The job was for Europe since 1500," I said. "But excluding specialists in France, Russia, Central Europe, the British Isles and Scandinavia."

"My God, what's left?"

"The Mediterranean and the Balkans."

"It's the Balkanization of our discipline."

"So I lied. In my application I told them about my minor with Bardoni and how I was planning a follow-up study of dueling and honorific codes in Mediterranean cultures."

"Did they buy it?"

"I got the interview, didn't I? But they also wanted an additional competence in Latin American history."

"I wasn't aware you possessed that competence."

"I taught two semesters of world history where we did the Spanish colonial empire, so thought I could slide by on that."

"Did it slide by in the interview?"

"Doubtful."

"When your book comes out in the summer I'm sure things will turn around. I've contacted all my people. Just hang on another year, can you promise me that?"

I promised.

Next day I had breakfast with my Nobleton editor Deborah Joliet. It was our first face-to-face meeting and she was extremely nice. We spoke very little of the book, for which I was grateful, and mostly about the baby she was expecting and how overwhelmed she was with manuscripts. Then I bolted to a fourth interview I had snagged at the last minute. Unscheduled as it was, my lunch with Deborah had me running late, and I dashed to the Hilton's Yosemite Room and hustled over to table F-7 where a man and woman were seated.

"Sorry about the delay," I said. "I was meeting with my publisher and lost track of time."

Neither of them offered their hand, let alone rose from their chair, so they loved me already.

"Please have a seat."

Ten minutes later they hadn't posed any questions about my scholarly work.

"Dr. McIlhenny, we're a teaching college," said the woman. "And I hope you understand that."

"Oh, yes."

"Which means that our main emphasis is pedagogy. It's not just a duty but a vocation – and we expect this attitude from all our faculty."

Where was this headed? I was an appalling teacher but had solid credentials.

"You're quite well published, three books already," said the guy. "I'm sure you know that the majority of American history professors never publish a single book their entire career. At our institute teaching would naturally consume the lion's share of your time, while your research and scholarship would take a definite backseat."

"Understandably."

"It just seems to us," said the woman finally lowering the boom, "that you're the type who'll be producing a book every five years."

What could you say to that?

Oh no, more like a book every six years, most assuredly not five, though with certain exceptions of course, like the editing jobs, and how about a harmless little textbook now and then, strictly in the cause of pedagogy, mind you . . .

42

On the return trip I flew into Paris since I needed to cross-check some things for my chapter on the French duel before submitting the final manuscript to Nobleton. I found a cheap place in the rue du Cardinal-Lemoine and trooped over to the Bibliothèque Nationale each day and otherwise kept a low profile. One fellow I saw on a daily basis was a *clochard* directly across the street from the hotel. Each morning he brought a folding chair and set it up near a trash receptacle, placed a porkpie hat on the pavement, lit a cigarette, crossed his legs and waited for business. He was gray-haired, gray-bearded and handsome. Not badly dressed. No wine or beer bottles in view. Gaelle's type of guy.

The sole person I met with was Oliver. We didn't rendezvous in the St.-Sulpice bar but on the Île St.-Louis. The place he had chosen was a café tucked into a cobblestone ruelle that only allowed for foot traffic. In waiting for him I drank *un blanc sec* and looked across the street at the old building with its top-floor garret windows in a mansard roof. Then I watched the pedestrians, my male gaze fixing on the well accoutered French girls with their slender bodies and delicate facial features and waxen wintry complexions that seemed without pores. Now there was an idea. Renting a garret on the Île St.-Louis and writing my novel and taking a girl like that as my mistress. She would revere my artistic talent, so not care about my domestic depredations, would find them endearing and even seductive, with a certain *épater le bourgeois* charm, and her ardent attentions would exhaust my sexual energies and keep my mind on work so I could live in the perfectly fulfilled present instead of always dreaming what some other condition might be like outside of academe . . .

"There he is – the German fifth column."

"Just a deserter."

"Churchill would have you shot."

"I'm a Yank, you limey."

"Reason enough."

He took a seat and ordered *un ballon de Beaujolais*. His accent speaking French was as atrocious as ever. I told him I'd been hanging with guilt-ridden Krauts and he allowed there was hope for me yet.

"So what's Gaelle's status?" I asked. "Has she taken up with some other guy?"

"Don't know, actually, she and Hélène haven't been in touch."

"Hope I wasn't the cause."

"You rate yourself pretty highly." He tapped the ash from his cigarillo and fixed me with an amused expression. "But not to worry. It was something between the two of them. You know how Frenchwomen can be."

"Testy?"

"That's a gallant way of putting it."

"You and Hélène get along okay."

"I'm an opportunist, old boy. The secret is knowing how to adapt. By the way she's pregnant, we're expecting in July."

I congratulated him and we toasted Beckett's grandson.

"So are you getting married now?"

"She hasn't asked me."

"But would you?"

"Given the right dowry."

43

Unsurprisingly, no on-campus interviews resulted from San Francisco, much less job offers. My Berlin fellowship would be running out in the summer, so I needed gainful employment locally, and it was Israel all over again.

After German reunification you had myriad language schools springing up. It seemed their clientele was mostly East Germans who felt or whose employers felt that they needed to finally learn English (the first foreign language taught in the GDR had been Russian) and I was hired by a school which sent me around East Berlin. My longest trip was to its far southeastern corner, in Friedrichshagen, at a scientific institute on the shore of a lake called Müggelsee. You got there by riding the S-Bahn for an hour, transferred to a streetcar which took you through a long stretch of conifer forest, from the final tram stop it was a fifteen-minute walk, and by the time you arrived it felt like you'd crossed over into Poland. My class consisted not of the scientists but the administrative staff. They were supposedly advanced beginners, so I gave my lessons completely in the target language as done at the Alliance Française, but to make absolutely sure they got my meaning I spoke with the painstaking clarity of Professor Higgins drilling Eliza Doolittle. I was using a textbook which had certain exercises.

"Ingeborg, let's start with you."

"Please."

"In this situation we don't say 'please' – you say 'please' for requests. That has nothing to do with the German word *bitte*. In our present situation you might say 'okay' or 'alright'."

"Ach ja natürlich!"

"So Ingeborg, let's start with you."

"Please."

"Ingeborg, do you like big dogs?"

"Oh yes, I like very much big dogs."

"I like big dogs *very much*."

"You like very much big dogs?"

"No, I mean, yeah, sure. But you say *you* like big dogs very much."

"You like very much big dogs."

"No. You say *I* like very much ... I mean ... just say it."

"Ich hab's schon zweimal gesagt, oder? You like very much big dogs."

"Okay, let's try Eckhard. Eckhard do you like whiskey?"

"Oh yes, I like very much whiskey."

"The more the better, huh? So you must like drinking."

"Yes, I like very much."

"Drinking."

"Drinking."

"The whole sentence please."

"Very much drinking I like yes."

"Okay, you like drinking very much – do you like eating?"

"Oh no, I dislike eating."

"You dislike eating?"

"Yes, very much."

"You never eat?"

"No, never."

"Eckhard, do you know what 'eating' means?"

"Yes, very much."

"So if I gave you a bratwurst you wouldn't take it?"

"I will pay it."

"But will you eat it?"

"Oh no."

"How do you live?"

"Rahnsdorfer Strasse 75."

It was often better to just ditch the textbook and engage in normal conversation. To get the students talking I might ask them how they had spent their weekend.

"Ingeborg, how did you spend your weekend?"

"My husband died."

"Oh, wow, hey . . . I'm really sorry . . . I mean . . . are you *okay?*"

"No."

"You don't have to be here, you know."

"I know."

"Anytime you want to go, just get up and leave, don't even ask permission."

"I stay."

"Great, uh, fine . . . sooo . . . Ingeborg's husband died . . . that's terrible news of course . . . but her use of the simple past tense was very well done since it's a completed action in the past . . . as death typically is . . . though she might also have used the present perfect tense because it's a very recent event: *My husband has died . . .*"

44

Then I got a reprieve from English-teaching. In a way. Since it was still teaching, and in East Berlin, but this time at a place called Waldo International University. They needed someone to fill in for a course in world history because the previous teacher had died suddenly, everyone was dying, and when I arrived at the Waldo building the place itself was dead. In the musty lobby the only sign of life was an old guy in a lawnchair at a cardtable. I figured him for the custodian.

"Waldo International?"

"Fourth floor," he said not looking up from his soccer magazine.

"Is there an elevator?"

He jerked his thumb over his shoulder.

At the fourth floor there was no one else in the corridor and I heard no voices, not even muffled ones from behind what I assumed were classroom doors. I was looking for the dean's office, but so far the "university" was devoid of any distinguishing features save the stiff odor of janitorial disinfectant. Then I came to an open door and saw a matronly blond seated at a desk with a partially eaten soft pretzel on a napkin in front of her. She had a fingernail wedged in her teeth, apparently trying to pick out some pretzel, and on seeing me she withdrew her finger and her mouth went askew and her tongue pursued the operation behind closed lips. We stared at each other for a couple seconds, then either she got the nagging morsel with her tongue or felt she just couldn't keep me waiting any longer.

"May I help you?"

"I have an appointment with Mary Kachinsky."

She stood up and rapped on the communicating door of the adjacent office and went in. I heard voices. She came out.

"Ms. Kachinsky will see you now."

I walked past her through the door, her tongue still working behind pursed lips.

"Hello, I'm Mary Kachinsky," said a woman with short salt-and-pepper hair who rose from behind a desk that was empty except for a pen set on a spotless green blotter. We shook hands and she motioned me to a chair. "It's good of you to come at such short notice."

"I got wind of things through my institute," I said. "It sounds like you're in a bind."

"Yes," dropping her eyes and lowering her voice. "Dr. Muggridge passed on very suddenly. It came as a complete surprise to us all. He was only in his fifties, a devastating blow, to both the university and its students, he won't be easily replaced, an outstanding educator and even better man . . ." She said all the right things then finished by giving the armrests a bouncy little pat with her palms. "But what's over is over. Tell us something about yourself – background, teaching experience – one thing I know is that you're a scholar of some attainment."

I ran through my teaching credentials, stressing that world history was both my passion and specialty, then she explained that Waldo was a global nexus of English-language universities whose units could be transferred to any U.S. college. The Berlin arm of Waldo's international network was only in its second year of existence, primarily a business school, but it sought to ensure that its students received a broad liberal-arts education. We discussed certain particulars including payment and the grading system, she gave me a course syllabus to examine, I expressed my satisfaction, and we hammered out a deal right then and there.

"By the way," I asked as she escorted me to the door. "How many students do I have?"

"Five."

"Five?"

"We're still in our start-up phase, as I told you, but recruitment is gaining momentum. I think next semester we should double that figure."

It turned out there were only five students in the whole *university,* and since this was the sole history course on offer, I composed a proud faculty of ONE. As it also happened, three of the five students were black. I was looking forward to putting all this in my next job application stateside: *I am currently teaching at a majority-black college in Berlin where I am also the acting departmental head . . .*

45

I was keeping late hours at the institute, compiling my book's index, which you left for last and was a tedious hassle, and after everyone had gone home I would head for the cellar where they stored multiple crates of beer for the conferences and other functions. They had different brands but I mainly imbibed the Radeberger Pils, like in the old days when I was doing dissertation research in East Berlin, and it put the taste of productivity in my mouth. I usually got out of there before midnight to catch the last bus home, but sometimes I just lined up the cushioned chairs and went to sleep, sort of romantic if you think about it, the overworked scholar heroically plowing through final revisions of his magnum opus before collapsing in exhaustion on the makeshift bed with his rolled-up London Fog as a pillow.

The institute's director didn't see it as romantic.

I was always careful to bring each beer bottle back down to the cellar and insert it in the empties crate before grabbing another one, so there was never any *visible* evidence, but it wasn't hard to guess what I'd been up to when my boss saw me lying there one morning smelling like a brewery.

"Guten Morgen, Herr McIlhenny, putting in long hours?"

"Looks like it."

"We're in Germany, not Japan," his comparative mind ever humming away. "Overtime really isn't necessary."

"I missed the last bus."

"They're running again if you want to go home for some rest."

"I'm pretty rested at this point – I think I'll get back to work."

And did.

A week later I sent off the completed index and final proofs to Nobleton.

Five years of steady application and now done.

For the next few days I went on a tear. One night I ended up in a Kreuzberg dive called the Bambara Bar, they were playing funk music, and I was sole white guy in the place. There were a number of white women, but the other males were black Africans by the look of things. I went to the bar and ordered a beer.

"Dr. McIlhenny!"

Down the bar were my three black students – Jessica the pretty American girl, Lucinda the Jamaican woman, and Bertrand the kid from Sierra Leone.

"What brings you all here?" I said. "Why aren't you home studying?"

"What brings *you* here?"

"I need a drink."

"We're here to dance!"

"Don't let me stop you."

"We're waiting for better music."

I pulled up a barstool. "So Bertrand, old boy, you're on the town with these two beautiful women. What have you got that I don't got?"

"I am a charming man!"

"Is that right ladies?"

"Oh yes!" said butterball Lucinda.

"Then I guess I'll have to take lessons from Bertrand."

"One lesson I can't give you," he said. "How to change your skin color!"

"Whoo-hoo-hoo!" crowed Lucinda.

"Hey, that's below the belt," I said.

"You're right," said Bertrand, "I *mean* below the belt!"

Another loud whoop from Lucinda. Jessica was giggling too. Chesty little guy this Bertrand.

"Come on, boys and girls," I said. "Let's keep it clean."

"We're clean," said Bertrand. "I mean the *legs*. Sprinting. It's in our genes. All the American slaves were from West Africa, that's why American blacks are so fast."

"Don't forget Jamaica, mon!" said Lucinda.

"Then why aren't the West Africans fast?" said Jessica.

"We're fast too," said Bertrand.

"Did you run track?" I asked.

"In high school I ran the 100 and 200."

"I was a quarter man," I said. "But bet I can still take you in a 60-yard dash."

"WHOO-HOO-HOO!"

"Bet you can't."

"Bet I can."

"Bet you can't."

"Just one way of settling it."

"You want to *race*?"

"Sure."

"When?"

"No time like the present."

"WHOO-HOO-HOO!"

We left our drinks and walked outside. The street in front of the Bambara was dead to traffic and had a slight upward grade. Jessica walked the acclivity, pacing off the yardage, then stood in the light of a streetlamp to mark the finish.

"It's more like 80 yards!" she called down. "Just so you can see me!"

"The longer the better!" I yelled back.

Lucinda had stayed with me and Bertrand to act as starter. He slipped off his shoes and socks, while I kept mine on. He did some toe-touches and threw in a couple more stretching exercises.

"On your marks!"

He got down on all fours as if lowering into starting blocks. I assumed a slight crouch.

"Go!"

It caught me unprepared, maybe Bertrand too, since we took off together. Then he nosed ahead, but I picked up momentum and drew even, and we stayed like that for a couple seconds until I finally churned past him and crossed the finish line in front. Jessica was hooting with excitement.

"Best two out of three?" I said shaking Bertrand's hand. "Lucinda forgot to say 'set'."

He begged off. And seemed a little shocked. A guy who takes off his shoes and lowers into a sprinter's crouch is bent on WINNING.

"But I demand a rematch!" he said back in the Bambara. "When we're sober and rested."

"You mean when *you're* sober and rested."

"WHOO-HOO-HOO-HOO-HOO!"

In the remaining weeks of that semester I can't say I ever saw Bertrand less than stone sober in class, but he apparently never felt rested enough for that rematch.

46

In late summer my book was published. Nobleton took out a big ad in America's most famous literary review and my first critique was a full page in Europe's most prestigious one: *The London Literary Gazette*. The critique was authored by a distinguished British historian and was both good and bad. He thought the book had many virtues (he particularly liked the chapter on the duel's mechanics and protocol, which had been my maiden effort at writing while smashed) but he also felt my prose was an affront to good taste and the prescriptions that govern historical writing. This was the basic paradox of the other reviews as well. My treatment held them in thrall yet they were troubled by a non-academic writing style that, to my way of thinking, was precisely what made for that enthralling treatment to begin with. But I forgave them. They weren't accustomed to serious scholarly work conjoined with moxie and zing and colloquial language. They hadn't gotten the memo that the 21st century was looming and their kind of stuffed-shirt writing a thing of the past. Deborah Joliet had gotten it, the Nobleton Board of Trustees had gotten it, and the reviews kept pouring in. That the *Literary Gazette* had considered the book at all was terrific, but getting into the act were *The Wall Street Journal*, *The Economist* and *The Guardian* among others, then came the academic journals, and after a couple months it amounted to some forty write-ups which were overwhelmingly positive, many quite sterling, and then that holy of holies, the *NAH Quarterly*, consecrated my effort with an admiring critique which ended on the plain and simple words: "This book merits an enduring place in the historical canon of modern Germany."

In November came a fax from Deborah saying that Nobleton had already sold 2000 books, which meant that even if they didn't unload another copy I would still have a nice royalty check next year. In her fax Deborah added that my paper on German student dueling had been a big hit at the recent stateside meeting of the Cultural History Association and that a number of people had come to the Nobleton booth afterward for my book. The paper was my contribution to a panel on dueling and was read *in absentia* since I couldn't afford the plane fare.

I was going to need those royalties.

Deborah had sent the fax to the Institute for Modern Comparative History, which was permitting me to keep it as my mailing address. This was crucial in applying for professorships, my fifth go-round with this nonsense, and that fall the NAH newsletter had 157 history jobs listed. Yet only seven or eight were positions for which I was solidly qualified, five were slots for which I was somewhat qualified, so it was me and hundreds of others battling for a dozen posts. Especially ominous was a certain rider that in years past had been typically appended to jobs in African-American History, Women's History, Latin American History, Middle Eastern History, Sub-Saharan African History, Native-American History, East Asian History – which themselves were increasing in number while the European jobs were growing less –

but now that rider was everywhere you looked: *The department has a commitment to cultural diversity and actively seeks and strongly encourages applications from members of visible minorities and traditionally under-represented groups, including women, aboriginal peoples, other persons of color, and those with disabilities.*

My only disability was that I didn't have one; the sole minority to which I belonged was that minuscule and ever shrinking group of people in academe who didn't give a damn about Michel Foucault.

A number of ads also sported another rider that had become more persistent: *pending final budgetary approval.* One of these was for a job where Jeremy was on the faculty. Before wasting time in applying for it, I called my old Yalom Eldad roommate to ask just what the chances of that final budgetary approval might be.

"Pretty good," he said. "And you're talking to the right boy since I'm on the search committee."

"And you only tell me *now?*"

"Steve, they're looking for a woman."

"How come that doesn't surprise me."

"It's out of our control."

"The administrators?"

"Word straight from the top."

"So a losing battle."

"Believe me, baby, I'm doing you a favor."

I still sent out twenty applications and had Deborah mail complimentary copies of my book to the search committees of the five most desirable schools, and of those twenty applications the number of interviews I landed for Chicago was exactly none.

47

In the meantime Waldo had folded operations. When you have more profs than students, something has to give. Their meatball operation had straggled along for two years but simply couldn't make ends meet. I knew the feeling. Now I had no income, even of a meager sort, along with no immediate prospects and dwindling cash reserves. To avoid a return to English teaching, I got a job working for an agency that gave historical walking tours of Berlin. Like the language schools, a lot of these agencies had sprung up after unification. In my application I naturally stressed my German-history credentials, but they seemed most impressed by my stint one summer giving tours at an animal sanctuary for endangered species called Cageless Critters.

My assignment the first day out was to take American tourists through downtown Berlin. This was plain sailing – Unter den Linden, the Reichstag, the Brandenburg Gate – but then I ran into trouble. The problem was that at top of the tour I had promised them Hitler's bunker, somewhere near Voss and Wilhelmstrasse, while overlooking the fact that the city fathers were in the process of rebuilding this bombed-out section where the Wall and deathstrip had also been and which was now one massive construction site.

"Wait here a moment," I told my group and went over to a nearby currywurst stand. The proprietor wore a white smock so full of ketchup and mustard stains, along with grease and other drippings, that it looked like a priceless Jackson Pollock painting.

"I'm giving a tour of Berlin to American tourists," I said. "You wouldn't know where Hitler's bunker is?"

He stared at me.

"It was beneath the Reich Chancellery," I explained. "Which according to my information is right about here, but I want to know exactly."

"Huh?"

"Der Bunker," I repeated. "Der *Führer*bunker."

"Bunker? What bunker?"

"Okay, make it a large Schultheiss."

I killed the beer, belched, and walked back to my group.

"Ladies and gentlemen, next stop Hitler's bunker!"

"Oh great!"

"A real photo-op!"

We walked along as I scanned this terra incognita. There were giant craters and mounds of debris and everywhere you looked were cranes.

"Okay folks, there are no official markers since the government doesn't want the site becoming a place of pilgrimage for neo-Nazis . . ."

I spied an acceptable candidate. It was a sunken concrete slab with rusty metal rods shooting upward and otherwise strewn with cylindrical chunks of cement. If you used your imagination – and mine was going full throttle – it might be construed as smashed pill-boxes or a last-stand defensive position.

"... but if you look right here you can get a glimpse into the inner sanctum of the totalitarian monolith, that command post and nerve center of the Nazi infamy: Hitler's bunker. He holed up here while the Third Reich fought its final battle against the advancing Red Army. Just thirty feet below that innocuous-looking slab lies a labyrinth of tunnels and secret chambers, like an ant colony of reinforced concrete, where the SS body-guards sacrificed themselves to serve and protect their Führer, who committed suicide on April 30th, 1945, ten days after his fifty-sixth birthday, in the conviction that Germany had not only failed but betrayed him."

Cameras clicked.

"Is there a passageway to it?" one person began the questioning. "Can we go down and have a look?"

"Unfortunately no, after the war the entrance was sealed. The SS hats are still hanging from hooks on the wall, the bath towels with monogrammed swastikas are still neatly folded in their cabinets. Everything just as it was found."

"And Hitler's corpse?"

"Cremated."

"Where?"

"You see that charred area? Next to what looks like a toppled pillar?"

Cameras clicked.

"But were his remains ever recovered?"

"By the Russians."

"How did they know it was Hitler?"

"Through dental records."

"Is that all?"

"Well, maybe one other thing."

"What other thing?

"It's a bit indelicate . . ."

"Ah, come on."

"Hitler had only one testicle."

"What?"

"One ball."

"Jeezus."

"Evidently a goat bit it off when our aspirant dictator was just a tot. The research has made tremendous strides in recent years. In fact more than a few historians have attempted to trace the Holocaust back to this physical defect."

"Isn't that a little farfetched?"

"You know how blunt the teeth of a goat are?"

"No."

"By comparison a guillotine would have been downright humane."

One corner of the chainlink fence surrounding the site was damaged and a couple cageless critters from our group had squeezed through it and were starting down the dirt slope to the sunken slab – which might lead to certain unwished-for discoveries.

"Stop!" I yelled. "There could be undetonated aerial bombs down there!"

They hurried back the way they came.

"You never know what can explode here," I said. "Last month a blockbuster bomb was set off by a steam shovel digging right near this site. That's why it's fenced off, for your own protection."

"But what about them?"

Some hundred yards off a group of boys had snuck through the fence and were having a dirt-clod fight.

"Probably neo-Nazis," I shook my head sadly. "They're aware of the danger. There's nothing we can do."

"But they look like kids – "

"Okay folks! Next stop on our tour a real snakepit – the Topography of Terror – where the Gestapo had its headquarters and torture chambers!"

"Oh goody!"

"A real treat!"

I pointed them back down the Wilhelmstrasse and they scampered off with me bringing up the rear. After a few steps I altered my course and went over to the guy at the currywurst stand.

"We found it," I said. "Another large Schultheiss."

THE END

Selected Books from PalmArtPress

Kevin McAleer
Berlin Tango
ISBN: 978-3-96258-051-3
274 Pages, Novel, Softcover/Flaps, English

Kevin McAleer
Surferboy
ISBN: 978-3-96258-020-9
244 Pages, Novel, Softcover/Flaps, English

Kevin McAleer
Errol Flynn – An Epic Life
ISBN: 978-3-96258-005-6
394 Pages, Biography / Epic Poem, Hardcover with Dustjacket, English

Rüdiger Görner
The Marble Song
ISBN: 978-3-96258-079-7
280 Pages, Softcover/Flaps, English

Robert Brandts
As We Drifted – *Als wir dahin trieben*
ISBN: 978-3-96258-056-8
Translation: Mitch Cohen, Wolfgang Heyder
100 Pages, Poetry, English/German

Reinhard Knodt
Pain – Schmerz
ISBN: 978-3-941524-77-4
200 Pages, Short Prose, Softcover/Flaps, English/German

Christian Wingrove-Rogers
CLAY TREE BIRD
ISBN: 978-3-96258-080-3
68 Pages, Flash Fiction, Poetry, English

Dennis McCort
A Kafkaesque Memoir – *Confessions from the Analytic Coach*
ISBN: 978-3-941524-94-1
474 Pages, Softcover/Flaps, English

Jörg Rubbert
Beach Lovers
ISBN: 978-3-96258-046-9
157 Pages, Photography, Hardcover, English/German

Carmen-Francesca Banciu
Fleeing Father
ISBN: 978-3-96258-083-4
152 Pages, English

Sibylle Prinzessin v. Preussen, Friedrich Wilhelm Prinz v. Preussen
The King's Love – *Frederick the Great, His Gentle Dogs and Other Passions*
ISBN: 978-3-96258-047-6
Translation: Dennis McCort
160 Pages, Biography, Softcover/Flaps, English

Matéi Visniec
MIGRAAAAANTS! – *There's Too Many People on This Damn Boat*
ISBN: 978-3-96258-002-5
220 Pages, Theater Play, English/German

Reid Mitchell
Sell Your Bones
ISBN: 978-3-96258-022-3
100 Pages, Poetry, Softcover/Flaps, English

Alexander de Cadenet
Afterbirth – *Poems & Inversions*
ISBN: 978-3-941524-59-0
64 Pages, Poetry/Art, Softcover/Flaps, English

John Berger
garden on my cheek
ISBN: 978-3-941524-77-4
Paintings by Liane Birnberg
60 Pages, Poetry/Art, Softcover/Flaps, English

Sara Ehsan
Bestimmung – **Calling**
ISBN: 978-3-96258-065-0
160 Pages, Poetry, German/English